# Bloodbound Desire

Corinna Kelly

Published by Corinna Kelly, 2024.

This is a work of fiction. Similarities to real people, places, or events are entirely coincidental.

BLOODBOUND DESIRE

**First edition. October 6, 2024.**

Copyright © 2024 Corinna Kelly.

ISBN: 979-8227602053

Written by Corinna Kelly.

# Bloodbound Desire

In a world where darkness reigns and danger lurks in every shadow, love can be the most perilous force of all. Bloodbound Desire takes readers on a thrilling journey through the tangled web of forbidden romance, power, and destiny.

At the heart of the story is Lila, a young woman whose life changes forever after a fateful encounter with Viktor, a mysterious and captivating vampire. Drawn to his magnetic charm, she is soon pulled into a world of ancient secrets, dangerous rivalries, and a bond that defies the laws of both vampires and humans. As their connection deepens, Lila and Viktor must navigate the treacherous path of their Bloodbound relationship—a rare, eternal bond that ties their fates together in ways neither of them can fully control.

But love in the vampire world comes with high stakes. Caught between rival clans, the wrath of the Vampire Council, and the weight of their growing feelings, Lila and Viktor must decide how much they are willing to sacrifice for each other. Can love truly conquer all when the cost could be their lives—or worse, their humanity?

With danger around every corner and passion burning between them, Bloodbound Desire is a story of love that transcends the boundaries of life and death, light and darkness. For Lila and Viktor, being bound by blood means risking everything—for a love that may be both their salvation and their undoing.

Prepare to be swept into a world where love is powerful, eternal, and bound by blood.

# Chapter 1: A Dangerous Encounter

The night air was crisp, carrying with it the scent of pine and the faint echo of laughter from the distant heart of the city. Lila James pulled her jacket tighter around her as she walked down the empty street, the rhythmic sound of her boots on the pavement the only noise in the silence. It was the kind of night that felt alive with possibilities, a strange energy buzzing in the air, but she wasn't quite sure why.

She had just left a small café where she had met up with her best friend, Emma. Their usual Thursday night catch-up had been enjoyable enough, filled with laughter and light conversation, but something had felt off about the evening. There had been a strange tension in the air, though Lila couldn't put her finger on it. It was almost as if she had been waiting for something to happen, an unease lingering just beneath the surface.

It didn't help that she had chosen to walk home instead of calling a cab. The city streets were unusually deserted, making her feel even more exposed. She knew she should have listened to Emma's protests about walking alone at night, but stubbornness was something Lila prided herself on. She could take care of herself, or so she believed.

As she turned a corner onto a quieter street lined with trees, a sense of being watched prickled at the back of her neck. Lila slowed her pace, her instincts sharpening as her heart rate quickened. She cast a glance behind her but saw no one. The shadows stretched long in the glow of the streetlights, but they were empty. Still, the feeling persisted, crawling up her spine.

She quickened her steps, her fingers gripping her phone tightly in her pocket, ready to dial for help if necessary. The eerie quiet of the street amplified her racing thoughts. It wasn't fear, exactly—more like a heightened sense of awareness. She had always been intuitive, able to sense things just beyond the ordinary, but tonight felt different.

The wind picked up, rustling the leaves overhead. That's when she saw him—standing at the edge of the sidewalk just ahead, leaning casually against a lamppost as if he'd been waiting for her. The stranger was tall, his figure partially obscured by the shadows, but even from a distance, Lila could tell there was something... different about him.

His presence commanded attention in a way she couldn't explain. The man's posture was relaxed, but there was an intensity about him that set her nerves on edge. His eyes, though half-hidden in the dim light, seemed to pierce through the night, focused directly on her.

Lila hesitated, her feet faltering as her gaze locked with his. There was something magnetic about him, something that drew her in despite the warning bells going off in her mind. She forced herself to keep moving, though every instinct told her to turn around. The distance between them closed rapidly, and she could see him more clearly now.

The man had an otherworldly beauty—sharp, angular features that seemed too perfect for reality. His hair was a dark, silky mess that fell just past his ears, framing his pale skin. And then there were his eyes—dark, fathomless pools that held secrets she couldn't begin to comprehend. Lila's breath caught in her throat as she walked past him, her heart hammering in her chest.

But he didn't move. Not at first.

"Out a bit late, aren't we?" His voice was low, smooth, and unsettlingly calm.

Lila stopped, her body tensing at the sound. She glanced over her shoulder, meeting his gaze once more. Something in his eyes flickered—a brief flash of amusement, or perhaps curiosity. She couldn't tell. But she wasn't the kind of person to be intimidated easily, and this stranger, no matter how unsettling, wasn't going to scare her.

"I could say the same about you," Lila replied, her voice steady despite the tightness in her chest.

The man pushed himself off the lamppost, taking a single step closer. The movement was so fluid, so graceful, that it almost seemed unnatural. Lila took a step back, instinctively widening the gap between them, though her feet felt glued to the ground.

"You shouldn't be out here alone," he said softly, almost like a warning.

Her heart raced, but she squared her shoulders, forcing herself to stand tall. "I can handle myself, thanks."

The corner of his mouth lifted slightly in what could have been a smile, though it didn't quite reach his eyes. He tilted his head, studying her with an intensity that made her feel exposed, vulnerable. "You're not like the others, are you?" he murmured.

Lila's stomach twisted. The way he spoke, as if he knew something about her that she didn't—it unnerved her. "What's that supposed to mean?"

Before he could answer, something shifted in the air, and a gust of wind rushed down the street, colder than before. Lila shivered, pulling her jacket tighter. The man's expression hardened, and he glanced down the street, his posture becoming rigid.

"You need to leave," he said suddenly, his voice losing its previous calm.

"What?" Lila asked, confused by the abrupt change in his demeanour.

"Now," he urged, stepping toward her. His tone was no longer casual; it was urgent. "Get out of here."

Lila blinked, her heart thundering in her chest as the tension between them reached a breaking point. Every instinct screamed at her to run, to get as far away from this strange man as possible, but something kept her rooted in place. She wasn't sure if it was curiosity or fear, but she couldn't seem to move.

"Lila."

The sound of her name caught her completely off guard. She hadn't told him her name. Her stomach churned as panic gripped her. How did he know?

Before she could speak, there was a sudden blur of movement, faster than her eyes could track. The man lunged forward, grabbing her wrist and pulling her to the side just as something crashed onto the pavement where she'd been standing moments ago.

Lila gasped, her mind struggling to process what had just happened. Her body reacted on instinct, pulling away from him, but he held her tight, his eyes scanning the street as if searching for something unseen.

"What the hell is going on?" she demanded, her voice shaky.

The man's gaze flicked back to her, and for the first time, Lila saw a flicker of something behind his eyes—concern. "There's no time to explain. You're in danger."

Her pulse raced. Danger? From what? She looked down at the shattered pavement where she had been standing. Whatever had caused it wasn't natural.

"Trust me," he said quietly, his grip on her wrist loosening slightly. "I'll keep you safe, but you need to listen to me."

Lila's heart pounded as adrenaline surged through her veins. Everything in her screamed to pull away, to run, but something about him—despite the fear, despite the confusion—made her believe him.

"What are you?" she asked, her voice barely above a whisper.

He hesitated, the tension between them thick enough to cut through. His dark eyes met hers, and for a brief moment, the façade of mystery and control fell away, revealing something deeper, more dangerous.

"A vampire," he whispered, his voice soft but certain.

Lila's breath caught in her throat. She wanted to laugh, to call him crazy, but the way he looked at her, the way her instincts screamed that something was different about him—it all came crashing down. The strange energy, the unnerving presence, the impossible speed.

Everything made sense.

And nothing made sense.

Before she could react, the sound of footsteps echoed from the shadows, and Viktor—he finally gave her his name—turned to face the approaching threat. Lila's world had just been upended, and now, it seemed, it was only going to get darker.

# Chapter 2: Crimson Shadows

The world around Lila had shifted in ways she couldn't fully comprehend. One minute she had been walking home from a simple night out with a friend, and the next, her reality had been upended by a stranger—a man, a vampire, named Viktor. The cold, calculating danger in his eyes hadn't scared her as much as the truth he had revealed.

A vampire. Lila still couldn't bring herself to fully believe it, but the evidence was impossible to deny. His unnatural speed, the strength with which he had pulled her away from whatever force had shattered the pavement beneath her feet, and the way the air seemed to hum with something unearthly around him—it was all too real. Yet none of it made sense.

Now, only hours after their encounter, Lila found herself pacing the small living room of her apartment, her mind racing to make sense of everything. She couldn't stop thinking about him—the vampire. His name echoed in her mind: Viktor. What was it about him that made her feel both drawn and terrified at the same time?

Her phone buzzed, pulling her out of her thoughts. It was a message from Emma.

Emma: Did you make it home safe? You were acting weird tonight.

Lila stared at the text for a moment, debating how to respond. She couldn't exactly explain what had happened. There was no way she could tell Emma about Viktor, about vampires, or about the strange attack that had almost ended her life. Emma would think she'd lost her mind.

Lila: Yeah, just tired. I'll call you tomorrow.

She set the phone down, her thoughts immediately returning to Viktor. The urgency in his voice when he had told her she was in danger replayed in her mind. Who—or what—had attacked her last night? And why had Viktor intervened? If he was a vampire, wasn't he supposed to be the one she should fear?

A knock at her window made her jump. Lila's heart raced as she turned to look, her pulse pounding in her ears. Standing outside her fire escape, shrouded in shadows, was Viktor.

Her breath caught in her throat. How had he gotten up to her third-floor apartment without making a sound? She swallowed hard, her hand trembling as she moved toward the window. Against every instinct that told her to leave him out there, she unlatched it and pushed it open.

"You shouldn't be here," she said, her voice shaky but firm.

Viktor stepped into the room with fluid grace, his movements far too smooth to be human. He didn't answer her immediately, his dark eyes scanning the room before finally settling on her. There was something different about him now—less threatening, perhaps, but still just as dangerous.

"I told you, you're not safe," Viktor replied, his voice low and calm. "They'll come for you again."

"Who's they?" Lila asked, her heart pounding in her chest. "And what the hell do they want from me?"

He sighed, crossing the room in a single, swift movement that left her breathless. "There's a war brewing, Lila. Between vampire clans. You're caught in the middle of it, and you don't even know why."

"Why me?" she demanded, her voice louder than she intended. "I'm just a regular person. I don't have anything to do with vampires or your world."

Viktor's expression hardened, as if he knew something he wasn't telling her. "You're more connected to this world than you realize."

Lila's stomach churned. What was that supposed to mean? "What are you talking about? You're not making any sense."

"Look," Viktor said, his tone softening. "The attack on you last night wasn't random. There are vampires—dark ones—who want something from you. I don't know what it is yet, but I'm going to find out."

Lila stared at him, her mind reeling. The idea of being the target of vampire assassins was surreal, but the seriousness in Viktor's voice left no room for doubt. "How do you even know all of this?"

"Because I've been watching you." His confession was blunt, and Lila felt a cold chill run down her spine. "I've kept my distance, but when I realized they were closing in, I had no choice but to intervene."

"Watching me?" Lila's voice wavered. "Why?"

Viktor stepped closer, his gaze intense. "You're in more danger than you think. The vampires who attacked you last night are from a clan called the Crimson Shadows."

"The Crimson Shadows," Lila repeated, the name sending a shiver through her. "What do they want with me?"

Viktor hesitated, as if weighing how much to reveal. "The Crimson Shadows are a ruthless vampire clan, notorious for their cruelty. They seek power at any cost, and they believe you're the key to something they want."

Lila's head spun. "But I don't even know any vampires. I'm not part of this world."

"You may not realize it, but there's something about you that makes you valuable to them," Viktor said, his voice steady. "I don't know what it is yet, but I do know this: if they get their hands on you, they'll use you to gain power—power that could tip the balance between vampire clans."

Lila's breath quickened. "So what am I supposed to do? Just hide forever?"

Viktor's gaze softened, and for the first time since their meeting, Lila saw a hint of vulnerability in him. "I won't let that happen. I'll protect you."

She wanted to believe him, but the reality of the situation was too overwhelming. Vampires. Clans. Blood wars. And now, somehow, she was a target in the middle of it all. It was too much.

"Why?" she asked quietly, looking up at him. "Why would you risk your life for me?"

Viktor's jaw tightened, and he stepped even closer, close enough that she could feel the coldness of his presence. "Because I know what it's like to be hunted."

The weight of his words hung between them. Lila had so many questions, but there was one thing she couldn't ignore—Viktor had saved her life. Twice now. And as much as she wanted to pretend that she could handle this on her own, deep down, she knew she needed his protection. But accepting that meant trusting him, and she wasn't sure she was ready for that.

"What do we do now?" she asked after a long silence.

"We need to leave," Viktor said. "Tonight."

"Leave?" Lila's voice rose in disbelief. "I can't just leave my life behind. I have friends, a job—"

"They'll come for you again," Viktor interrupted, his tone firm but not unkind. "If you stay here, you'll be putting everyone you care about in danger."

Lila's chest tightened. As much as she hated to admit it, he was right. The attack last night had been too close, too real. She couldn't risk someone she loved getting caught in the crossfire.

"Where would we go?" she asked, her voice small.

"I know a place," Viktor replied, his eyes darkening. "Somewhere the Crimson Shadows can't find us."

Lila hesitated, the weight of the decision pressing down on her. Could she really trust him? Could she trust a vampire?

"I need time," she said, her voice barely above a whisper.

"You don't have time, Lila," Viktor said quietly, his eyes locking with hers. "But I'll give you tonight. I'll be back before dawn. Decide then."

With that, he turned and disappeared through the window, as silently as he had come. Lila stood there, staring at the empty space where he had been, her mind racing with everything he had said.

Her world had changed in an instant, and now she was faced with a decision that could alter the course of her life forever.

As the moon hung high in the sky, casting its cold glow over the city, Lila couldn't help but feel the weight of the shadows closing in around her—the shadows that had become all too real.

And somewhere, lurking within those shadows, was a dangerous truth she had yet to uncover.

# Chapter 3: The Bite of Fate

The days after Viktor's midnight departure passed in a blur for Lila. Everything that once seemed so mundane, so rooted in normalcy, had been upended by the impossible reality that she now faced. The world of vampires, once a myth confined to books and films, had come crashing into her life. And the center of it all was Viktor, a figure of mystery, danger, and allure that she couldn't seem to shake, no matter how hard she tried.

Lila tried to resume her normal routine, pretending nothing had changed. But Viktor's words, his warnings, haunted her every step. And worse still, she couldn't stop thinking about him—his intense gaze, the way his presence filled the room with an electric charge, and the lingering question of what tied her to the dark world of vampires. She was supposed to be scared of him, and part of her was. But the other part—the part she couldn't explain—was drawn to him like a moth to a flame.

Emma had noticed her distraction, of course. They sat together at their favourite café, the one where they always met up for coffee after work. Lila stirred her cappuccino absentmindedly, her thoughts far from the conversation, while Emma chatted about something Lila could barely focus on.

"You haven't heard a word I've said, have you?" Emma asked, her voice laced with concern.

Lila blinked, snapping back to reality. "What? Oh, I'm sorry, Emma. I've just been... distracted."

Emma frowned, leaning forward in her seat. "You've been distracted for days now. What's going on, Lila? And don't tell me it's nothing, because I know you too well for that."

Lila hesitated. She had been deliberately vague about what had happened the night of the attack. How could she possibly explain any of it without sounding insane? But Emma's sharp gaze didn't waver. Her best friend knew something was up.

"I met someone," Lila admitted finally, her voice quiet.

Emma's eyes lit up with a mixture of curiosity and surprise. "Really? You're only just telling me this now? Spill!"

Lila shifted uncomfortably in her seat, her fingers tightening around the coffee cup. "It's... complicated."

"Complicated how?" Emma raised an eyebrow.

"He's... different," Lila said slowly, choosing her words carefully. "And I don't think I should be involved with him."

Emma leaned back, crossing her arms. "Different how? Is he married or something?"

"No, nothing like that," Lila said quickly, shaking her head. "It's just... I don't know how to explain it. He's dangerous, Emma. I think I should stay away, but I can't stop thinking about him."

Emma's expression shifted, concern filling her eyes. "Lila, if you think he's dangerous, you need to listen to that. I don't care how attractive or mysterious he is, you can't put yourself in harm's way for some guy."

Lila nodded, knowing her friend was right. But no matter how much sense it made, she couldn't deny the magnetic pull she felt toward Viktor. She had never felt anything like it before—something beyond reason or logic, a force that seemed to draw her closer to him even as it frightened her.

"Just be careful, okay?" Emma added, reaching across the table to squeeze Lila's hand. "You don't need some guy complicating your life, especially if there's even a hint of danger."

Lila smiled weakly, appreciating Emma's protective nature. "I'll be careful, I promise."

But even as she said the words, Lila knew they were hollow. She wasn't sure she could stay away from Viktor, not now that the wheels of fate had already been set in motion.

### Later That Night

Lila's apartment felt quieter than usual that night. The city hummed with its usual sounds outside her window—cars in the distance, a few muffled voices on the street—but inside, there was an oppressive stillness that only deepened her sense of isolation. She stood by the window, staring out at the world, wondering how long it would be before Viktor showed up again.

And then, as if summoned by her thoughts, she felt him before she saw him.

A flicker of movement in the shadows below. She knew it was him before she even looked. Viktor emerged from the darkness, his figure cutting a striking silhouette against the dim glow of the streetlamp. Her heart skipped a beat, and a rush of anticipation shot through her.

He was here.

Without hesitation, she opened the window and stepped onto the fire escape, her breath catching as she met his gaze. He moved like a predator, graceful and silent, his presence commanding the space around him.

"You shouldn't be here," Lila said softly, her words a whisper on the wind.

"I told you I would protect you," Viktor replied, his voice smooth and low. "I never break my promises."

Lila swallowed, the air between them thick with unspoken tension. "What do you want from me, Viktor?"

He paused, his dark eyes searching hers, and for a moment, Lila thought she saw something deeper—something vulnerable—beneath the cold, controlled exterior.

"I don't know," he admitted, his voice barely audible. "But I do know that you're in more danger than you realize. And I can't let them take you."

Lila took a step closer, her curiosity overpowering her caution. "Who are 'they'? The Crimson Shadows?"

Viktor nodded, his expression darkening. "They're not the only ones after you, Lila. There are forces at work that even I don't fully understand. But I do know one thing—your blood is different."

"Different?" Lila repeated, confused.

"There's a legend among vampires," Viktor continued, his gaze never leaving hers. "The Bloodbound. It's a rare bond that forms between a human and a vampire. It's said to grant power—immense power—when the bond is sealed. Your blood carries something... unique. And the Crimson Shadows want it."

Lila's mind reeled. A bond? Power? She had never imagined that her ordinary life could be tied to something so extraordinary, so dangerous.

"But why me?" she asked, her voice trembling.

"I don't know," Viktor said, his expression serious. "But if the Bloodbound exists, if we're somehow tied together by fate, then you'll be hunted until the bond is either sealed or destroyed."

Lila felt a chill run down her spine. "And what happens if the bond is sealed?"

Viktor hesitated, his eyes darkening. "If it's sealed, we become connected in ways that go beyond this world. Our lives, our fates—bound together. But there's a cost."

"A cost?" Lila asked, her pulse quickening.

"You would no longer be just human," Viktor said, his voice barely above a whisper. "You would become part of my world—forever."

Lila's heart pounded in her chest as the weight of his words sank in. The choice before her was unfathomable: stay human and risk being hunted, or embrace the dark world of vampires and forever be bound to Viktor, both in body and soul.

"I don't want this," she whispered, her voice breaking. "I never asked for this."

"I know," Viktor said, his tone softer now. "But we don't always choose our fate."

The wind stirred between them, carrying the scent of something ancient and powerful, as if the very air around them was charged with the weight of destiny. Lila could feel it—the pull, the connection between them growing stronger, drawing her toward him despite the danger.

Viktor stepped closer, his presence intoxicating, and Lila found herself unable to move, unable to pull away. His eyes bore into hers, and in that moment, the world around them faded away, leaving only the two of them in the darkness.

And then, with a gentle touch, Viktor reached for her hand, his fingers cold against her skin.

"If you choose this," he said quietly, "there's no going back."

Lila's breath caught in her throat. The choice, the weight of the unknown, hung heavy between them.

But as she looked into his eyes, the pull was undeniable. She was drawn to him—drawn to the danger, the mystery, the power of the Bloodbound.

And she knew, in that moment, that her life would never be the same.

# Chapter 4: Forbidden Attraction

The nights grew longer, and with each passing moment, Lila found herself sinking deeper into a world she had never known existed. Viktor's presence had become a constant in her life, as unavoidable as the moonlight filtering through her window each night. No matter how hard she tried to distance herself, the connection between them seemed to pull her closer, binding her fate to his in ways she couldn't understand—and perhaps didn't want to.

Viktor, for his part, was always nearby, always watching, but there was a guarded distance in his eyes, a restraint that left her with more questions than answers. There was an undeniable pull between them, one that Lila had never felt before—an attraction so intense it made her pulse quicken whenever he was near. But beneath that pull was a tension, a shadow of something darker.

She couldn't help but wonder if he felt it too.

Tonight, Lila found herself alone once more in her small apartment, the soft hum of the city outside barely cutting through her thoughts. She had taken to pacing, her mind racing with questions that had no answers. What did Viktor see in her? Why was she so connected to this strange world of vampires, and what exactly did this "Bloodbound" mean for her future?

There was a knock at her window, and Lila's heart skipped a beat. She already knew who it was.

Viktor stood outside on the fire escape, his figure cloaked in the shadows, but she didn't hesitate this time. She crossed the room in a few short steps and opened the window, letting the cool night air rush in as Viktor slipped inside with his usual graceful ease.

He didn't say anything at first. His dark eyes searched hers, and for a moment, Lila felt as if he could see straight through her, into the depths of her soul. There was always something unreadable about him—something guarded.

"You shouldn't keep coming here like this," she said quietly, her pulse quickening despite her words.

"I know," Viktor replied, his voice low and soft. "But I had to make sure you were safe."

"You always say that," Lila said, her frustration bubbling up. "But what does that even mean? Safe from what? From the Crimson Shadows? From other vampires?"

Viktor's jaw tightened, and he turned his gaze away, staring out the window into the night. "Safe from me."

The admission caught her off guard, and for a moment, Lila was silent, watching him as he stood there, the weight of his words hanging between them like a thick fog. His usually calm, collected demeanour seemed to crack, revealing something deeper—something vulnerable.

"What do you mean?" she asked, stepping closer. "Why would I need to be safe from you?"

Viktor hesitated, his hands clenched at his sides as if he were wrestling with something inside himself. When he finally spoke, his voice was barely above a whisper.

"You don't understand what I am, Lila," he said, his gaze dark and troubled. "You don't understand what I could do to you."

Her heart pounded in her chest, but she refused to back down. "Then explain it to me."

Viktor turned to face her, his eyes burning with an intensity that made her breath catch in her throat. "I'm a vampire, Lila. A predator. You are human—fragile, breakable. And the more time I spend with you, the harder it becomes to resist what I am."

Lila took a step closer, her heartbeat loud in her ears. "But you haven't hurt me."

"Not yet," Viktor replied, his voice tight. "But the more we're around each other, the more dangerous it becomes. The bond between us—it's getting stronger. I can feel it."

Lila's pulse raced. The Bloodbound. The connection between them that neither could deny. "So what does that mean? Why are we connected like this?"

Viktor shook his head, frustration flickering in his eyes. "It's not supposed to happen. Vampires and humans aren't meant to be together like this. It's forbidden for a reason."

"Forbidden?" Lila asked, her breath catching. "By who? The Vampire Council?"

"By every instinct that runs through me," Viktor said, his voice filled with both pain and desire. "Humans are fragile, Lila. One wrong move, one moment where I lose control, and..."

He trailed off, but Lila understood the unspoken words. He could kill her—easily. She had seen the strength in him, the power that simmered just beneath the surface. And yet, despite knowing the risks, despite knowing the danger he posed, she couldn't help the way her heart ached for him, the way she felt drawn to him in ways she couldn't explain.

Her throat tightened, and for a moment, neither of them spoke, the silence between them thick with unspoken words, desires, and fears.

"You don't want to hurt me," Lila said softly, her voice trembling. "I can see that."

Viktor's eyes darkened, his gaze locking with hers. "No. I don't. But that doesn't mean I won't."

Lila stepped closer, closing the distance between them. "Then why do you keep coming back? Why do you keep trying to protect me if I'm so dangerous for you to be around?"

Viktor's hands clenched at his sides, his jaw tight as if he were fighting a war within himself. When he spoke, his voice was raw, filled with both longing and restraint.

"Because I can't stay away."

The admission sent a shockwave through Lila's heart. She had known, deep down, that there was something between them—something neither of them could control. But hearing it aloud made it real, made the danger all the more tangible.

"I'm drawn to you," Viktor continued, his eyes never leaving hers. "The Bloodbound—this bond between us—it's growing stronger every day. And the closer we get, the harder it becomes to resist."

Lila's heart raced, her pulse quickening with every word. She wanted to reach out, to touch him, to bridge the gap that seemed to exist between them despite the closeness. But something held her back—fear, perhaps, or maybe the realization that once she crossed that line, there would be no turning back.

"What happens if you don't resist?" she asked, her voice barely above a whisper.

Viktor's eyes flashed with something dark, something dangerous. "I lose control. I give in to the hunger."

Lila swallowed, her throat tight. "The hunger for blood?"

Viktor nodded, his gaze burning into hers. "Yes. And something more."

Lila's breath caught in her throat. She knew what he meant. It wasn't just about blood—it was about the attraction between them, the undeniable pull that had been growing stronger with each passing day. The bond between them wasn't just physical; it was something deeper, something primal.

"And if you give in?" Lila asked, her voice trembling.

Viktor's expression was a mixture of desire and torment. "Then you would be mine."

The words sent a thrill through Lila's body, her skin tingling with the weight of what he was saying. She could feel it too—the bond, the pull, the desire that seemed to simmer beneath the surface of every glance, every touch. But with that desire came danger, a danger that Viktor was trying desperately to protect her from.

Lila took a shaky breath, her heart pounding in her chest. "What if I want that?"

Viktor froze, his eyes widening in shock. "You don't understand what you're saying, Lila. Being with me—it's not like anything you've experienced before. You would be bound to me, body and soul. You wouldn't just be a part of my world—you would become a part of me."

Lila's mind raced, but she couldn't deny the truth any longer. She was falling for him—deeply, irreversibly. Despite the danger, despite the risks, she couldn't turn away.

"I don't care," she whispered, her voice barely audible.

Viktor stared at her, his gaze intense, and for a moment, Lila thought he might give in. But then, with a pained expression, he stepped back, putting distance between them once more.

"I care," he said, his voice rough with emotion. "I care too much."

And with that, he turned and disappeared into the night, leaving Lila standing alone, her heart aching with the weight of what could never be.

# Chapter 5: Secrets of the Night

The night was thick with an eerie stillness, as if the very air held its breath in anticipation of something inevitable. Lila sat at her kitchen table, her fingers tracing the rim of her coffee mug absentmindedly. She hadn't seen Viktor in days—not since he had walked away from her, leaving her with more questions than answers. The silence between them was unsettling, but it was the pull she felt toward him that left her restless and confused.

The rational part of her knew she should stay away from him, that his world was full of danger, darkness, and things she couldn't hope to understand. But her heart, bound by that mysterious connection she could feel growing stronger every day, wasn't ready to let go. It was as if a piece of her was tethered to him, no matter how much distance he put between them.

A soft knock at the window broke the silence, and Lila's heart leaped into her throat. She knew who it was before she even looked.

Viktor stood outside on the fire escape, his figure bathed in the soft glow of the moon. He seemed to blend with the shadows, an otherworldly presence that set her pulse racing. She hesitated for only a moment before opening the window to let him in.

He slipped inside without a sound, moving with the fluid grace that had become so familiar to her. His eyes, as dark and unreadable as ever, met hers, and for a moment, neither of them spoke.

"You're here," Lila said quietly, more of a statement than a question.

"I told you I'd protect you," Viktor replied, his voice low. "Even if it means protecting you from myself."

Lila's breath caught. She wanted to ask him what he meant, but she already knew. He had made it clear—being with him was dangerous. The growing bond between them, the attraction she could no longer deny, put them both in danger. But what danger exactly? And why?

"Why is it so dangerous?" Lila asked, voicing the question that had been burning in her mind for days. "Why is this connection between us something you're so afraid of?"

Viktor sighed, his expression softening. He moved toward the kitchen table and sat down, the weight of his silence hanging between them before he spoke again.

"There are rules," he said slowly, as if choosing his words carefully. "Rules that govern my world—the world of vampires. Humans are meant to remain... separate. We can exist alongside them, feed from them if necessary, but we cannot form bonds. Not like this."

Lila frowned, leaning against the counter. "What kind of rules? And who enforces them?"

"The Vampire Council," Viktor replied, his voice heavy with an unspoken bitterness. "They oversee the clans, maintain order. They've kept the vampire world in check for centuries."

Lila stared at him, her mind struggling to piece together this strange, hidden world. "The clans?"

Viktor's eyes darkened, and for a moment, a flicker of something—anger, perhaps—passed over his face. "There are many vampire clans, each with their own territories, their own hierarchies. The Crimson Shadows, who have been hunting you, are one of the most dangerous. They're ruthless, driven by power, and willing to break every law that exists if it means gaining more."

Lila's stomach twisted. She had known there was danger surrounding her, but hearing Viktor speak about the vampire clans made it feel all the more real—and terrifying. "And what about you? Which clan are you from?"

Viktor hesitated, his jaw tightening. "I was once part of a clan. The Blackthorn. But that was a long time ago."

His words were laced with a weight of regret, and Lila couldn't help but sense there was more to the story. "You left?"

"I had no choice," Viktor said quietly, his gaze dropping to the floor. "My past... it's complicated."

Lila crossed the room and sat down across from him, her curiosity outweighing her fear. "Tell me."

For a long moment, Viktor was silent, as if wrestling with whether or not to share his past. But when he finally spoke, his voice was filled with a sadness she hadn't heard before.

"Vampires aren't born," he began, his gaze distant. "We're made. Every vampire was once human, and we are turned through a ritual—an exchange of blood. But the transformation comes with a cost. We lose pieces of ourselves, of our humanity."

Lila listened intently, her heart pounding in her chest.

"The Blackthorn Clan was known for its strength, its power," Viktor continued. "But with power comes ambition, and with ambition comes corruption. The clan began to lose sight of the rules, bending them, breaking them, to gain more control. I became... disillusioned with what we had become."

His voice tightened, and Lila could see the pain etched on his face.

"So, I left. I walked away from the clan, from everything I had known. But the Council doesn't look kindly on those who abandon their clans. And I've been hunted ever since."

Lila's breath caught. "Hunted? By who?"

"By the Council, and by the Crimson Shadows," Viktor said. "Both see me as a threat. The Council because I refuse to fall in line, and the Crimson Shadows because they believe I know secrets about their clan that could destroy them."

Lila's mind reeled. She had been pulled into a world far darker and more dangerous than she had imagined, and Viktor was right in the middle of it. "But what does this have to do with me?"

Viktor's eyes met hers, and for a moment, the intensity of his gaze took her breath away. "The Bloodbound."

Lila swallowed hard. He had mentioned the Bloodbound before, but she still didn't fully understand what it meant. "The bond between us?"

Viktor nodded. "It's rare—unheard of, even. A vampire and a human forming a bond like this. It's forbidden because it's dangerous, for both of us. If the Council finds out, they'll see it as a threat to their power. And if the Crimson Shadows discover it, they'll use it to manipulate us."

Lila felt a chill run down her spine. "But why me? Why now?"

"I don't know," Viktor admitted, his voice softening. "But what I do know is that the bond between us is growing stronger every day. And if it continues to grow, it will be impossible to break."

Lila's heart pounded in her chest, her thoughts spinning. The idea of being connected to Viktor in such a way was both terrifying and exhilarating. She felt the pull, the connection, and she couldn't deny that a part of her wanted to explore it—to embrace the bond, no matter the danger.

But at what cost?

"There's more," Viktor said, his voice low. "If the bond is fully formed, if we seal it... we'll be bound together for eternity. Your life, your fate, will be tied to mine."

Lila's breath caught in her throat. Eternity. The word hung heavy in the air between them. Could she really be tied to Viktor's world forever? Could she survive in a world where danger and darkness lurked around every corner?

"And if we don't seal it?" Lila asked quietly.

"Then we'll both be vulnerable," Viktor said. "The bond is incomplete right now, which means it can be exploited—by the Crimson Shadows, by the Council, by anyone who wants to use it against us."

Lila's mind raced. She had never asked for any of this. She had never wanted to be part of this dark, hidden world. But now that she was, she couldn't walk away. The bond between her and Viktor was real, undeniable, and it was pulling her deeper into his world with every passing day.

"So, what do we do?" Lila asked, her voice barely above a whisper.

Viktor's gaze darkened, and for a moment, Lila thought she saw a flicker of something dangerous in his eyes—something raw and primal.

"We fight," he said softly. "But first, we need to decide whether we're willing to take the risk."

"The risk of what?"

Viktor leaned closer, his voice low and filled with an intensity that made her heart race. "The risk of falling for each other."

Lila's breath caught, her pulse quickening. The forbidden attraction between them, the bond that tied them together—it was dangerous, but it was real. And in that moment, as Viktor's eyes burned into hers, she knew that no matter the consequences, she couldn't walk away.

Their fates were intertwined, bound by secrets, danger, and the undeniable pull of something far deeper than either of them could control.

# Chapter 6: The Blood Moon's Curse

The soft glow of the full moon filtered through the heavy curtains in Lila's apartment, casting eerie shadows across the room. Tonight, the moon seemed different—larger, redder, as if it had taken on a life of its own. The sight of it sent a shiver down her spine, a feeling of dread settling deep in her bones. She had heard Viktor mention the Blood Moon before, but she had never asked what it meant. Now, she wasn't sure she wanted to know.

The tension between her and Viktor had only grown since their last conversation. The revelation of the Bloodbound—the forbidden bond between human and vampire—had left Lila with more questions than answers. She had started to notice changes within herself: heightened senses, a strange awareness of Viktor even when he wasn't near. It was as though something inside her was waking up, something primal.

And then there was the curse. Viktor had been vague about it, but the warning in his voice had been enough to set her on edge. He had spoken of ancient vampire legends, curses tied to the Bloodbound, and the dangers they now faced because of their growing bond. But Lila wasn't one to sit idly by, waiting for fate to decide her future.

Determined to find answers, Lila had spent hours combing through old books she had found in a forgotten corner of an antique shop. The dusty pages spoke of legends, rituals, and vampire lore that stretched back centuries. One story, in particular, had caught her attention—a legend about the Blood Moon and the curse it carried.

Tonight, with the moon looming ominously outside her window, Lila felt compelled to dive deeper into the legend. She sat cross-legged on her bed, the ancient book open in front of her. The words were written in an old, faded script, barely legible, but Lila strained to make sense of them. Her heart pounded as she read the story of the Blood Moon's curse, the truth behind the bond that now tied her to Viktor.

The Blood Moon, the legend said, was a rare celestial event, occurring only once in a generation. Its crimson light was believed to awaken ancient forces, forces that could either grant immense power or bring about catastrophic ruin. It was under this moon that the Bloodbound bond could be sealed, binding a human and a vampire together for eternity.

But with that bond came a curse.

Lila's fingers trembled as she traced the faded words, her heart racing. The curse spoke of a love so powerful that it would consume those bound by it, a desire that would grow uncontrollable. While the bond granted strength and immortality to the human, it also brought danger—an insatiable hunger, a thirst that could only be quenched by blood.

As the bond deepened, the human would be drawn further into the vampire's world, losing pieces of their humanity. The hunger for blood, for power, would grow stronger, until it became impossible to resist. And in the end, one of them—either the human or the vampire—would be forced to make the ultimate sacrifice to break the curse.

Lila's blood ran cold as she finished reading the legend. She couldn't deny the truth behind the words. She had already begun to feel the pull of the bond—the strange connection to Viktor, the heightened senses, the overwhelming attraction that threatened to consume her. And now, with the Blood Moon rising, she feared that the curse was already taking hold.

Her mind spun with the implications. If the bond between her and Viktor continued to grow, if they gave in to their attraction, they would be bound together forever. But that bond came with a price—a price she wasn't sure she was willing to pay.

As if sensing her turmoil, there was a soft knock at the window. Lila's heart skipped a beat, and she knew without looking who it was. Viktor. He had been keeping his distance, but the pull between them was undeniable, and tonight, under the Blood Moon, she knew he wouldn't stay away.

She opened the window and let him in, the cool night air brushing past her as Viktor stepped inside. He looked different tonight—his usually composed expression was strained, his dark eyes flickering with something dangerous, something raw.

"You've felt it, haven't you?" Viktor said quietly, his voice low and intense. "The pull of the Blood Moon."

Lila swallowed, her heart pounding. "I've been reading about it. About the curse."

Viktor's jaw tightened, and he glanced out the window at the blood-red moon hanging in the sky. "The curse is real, Lila. The Bloodbound bond is powerful, but it's also dangerous. The more we're drawn to each other, the harder it will be to resist."

Lila stepped closer, her pulse quickening at the proximity between them. "What happens if we don't resist?"

Viktor's gaze darkened, his expression filled with both longing and regret. "If the bond is sealed under the Blood Moon, we'll be bound together forever. You'll be granted immortality, but you'll also inherit the hunger—the thirst for blood, for power. It will consume you, just as it consumes every vampire."

"And the curse?" Lila asked, her voice barely above a whisper.

Viktor's eyes flickered with something dark, something dangerous. "The curse states that one of us will have to make a choice—either you lose your humanity, or I lose control. One of us will have to sacrifice everything to break the bond."

Lila's breath caught in her throat. "Why didn't you tell me this sooner?"

"I didn't want to scare you," Viktor said softly, his gaze never leaving hers. "I thought I could protect you, keep you safe from the curse. But now…"

He trailed off, his eyes darkening with an emotion that sent a thrill through Lila's body. She could feel it—the pull between them, stronger than ever under the crimson light of the Blood Moon. It was as if the very air around them was charged with electricity, drawing them closer, binding them together in ways neither of them could resist.

"What do we do now?" Lila asked, her voice trembling with both fear and desire.

Viktor stepped closer, his presence overwhelming, his dark eyes burning with a mixture of longing and restraint. "We have to resist, Lila. If we give in, if we seal the bond tonight... there's no going back."

Lila's heart raced, her body aching to close the distance between them, to give in to the desire that had been simmering between them for so long. But Viktor's words echoed in her mind, a warning of the curse that loomed over them both.

She took a shaky breath, her hands trembling at her sides. "And if we don't give in?"

Viktor's gaze softened, his eyes filled with an emotion she couldn't quite place. "Then we fight the bond, fight the curse. But it will be harder than anything you've ever faced."

Lila stared up at him, her heart pounding in her chest. She knew he was right. The attraction between them, the connection that tied them together—it was undeniable. But the curse, the hunger, the danger... it was all too real.

"I don't know if I can resist," she whispered, her voice barely audible.

Viktor's jaw clenched, and for a moment, Lila thought he might give in, might close the distance between them and let the bond take hold. But then, with a pained expression, he took a step back, putting space between them once more.

"I'll help you," Viktor said, his voice rough with emotion. "We'll fight this together."

Lila's breath caught, and for the first time since their bond had begun to form, she felt a flicker of hope. They didn't have to give in to the curse. They didn't have to let the Blood Moon's power control their fate.

But as Viktor's eyes met hers, filled with both desire and restraint, she knew that the road ahead would be anything but easy.

The Blood Moon's curse was real, and it was already taking hold.

And now, as the night deepened and the moon's crimson glow bathed the world in its eerie light, Lila realized that the greatest battle they would face wasn't against the vampires hunting them.

It was against the desires growing inside them both.

# Chapter 7: Crossing the Line

Viktor stood at the edge of the rooftop, watching the city below as the soft glow of streetlights reflected off the rain-slicked pavement. The sky, once thick with the red hue of the Blood Moon, had faded back to its usual midnight blue, but its lingering effect hung over him like a shadow. The night felt heavier than usual, burdened with thoughts and desires he had long fought to suppress.

He had been standing there for hours, trying to distance himself from the very thing that occupied his every thought—Lila.

She was becoming more than just a human under his protection. She was becoming his weakness, a source of both solace and torment. Every instinct told him to walk away, to leave her behind before the bond between them grew any stronger, before the inevitable darkness of his world consumed her. Yet, no matter how hard he tried to convince himself, Viktor knew he couldn't stay away.

He had crossed a line.

The connection between them—the Bloodbound—was dangerous enough, but the feelings he had begun to develop for her were something altogether different. They were something no vampire should allow themselves to feel for a human. It was forbidden, not just by the laws of the Vampire Council, but by the very nature of what he was.

And yet, despite every rational reason to keep his distance, he found himself drawn back to her, night after night.

Viktor closed his eyes, trying to push away the memory of their last encounter. The way her eyes had met his, filled with fear and desire. The way her pulse had quickened when he had moved closer, the sound of her heartbeat flooding his senses. It had taken everything in him to step back, to resist the pull of the bond that seemed to grow stronger with every passing day.

But resisting was becoming harder.

He heard a soft noise behind him and turned to see Lila standing at the rooftop entrance, her eyes searching his face, her expression both hesitant and determined. His heart, or what was left of it, clenched at the sight of her. She had come looking for him, and part of him hated that he was glad to see her.

"Viktor," she said softly, stepping forward. "I was worried about you. You've been avoiding me."

He didn't answer right away, his jaw tightening as he fought the urge to close the distance between them. She had no idea how hard this was for him—how much he was fighting against everything inside him to keep her safe.

"I haven't been avoiding you," he said quietly, his voice rough. "I've been trying to protect you."

Lila took another step forward, her eyes never leaving his. "From what? Yourself?"

His breath hitched at her words, and for a moment, he couldn't bring himself to meet her gaze. She was right, of course. He was as much of a danger to her as the Crimson Shadows or any other vampire who wanted her blood. Maybe more so. His feelings for her made him unpredictable, made him weak.

But Lila wasn't the kind of person to back down. She moved closer, her presence warm and unsettling, and Viktor could feel the heat of her body even from where he stood. The desire to pull her into his arms, to give in to the bond that tied them together, was overwhelming.

"I know you're scared," she said softly, her voice filled with both understanding and determination. "But I'm not afraid of you, Viktor. You've saved me, more than once. You're not going to hurt me."

"You don't understand," Viktor said, his voice strained. "It's not about wanting to hurt you. It's about what happens if I lose control."

Lila's brow furrowed, but she didn't back down. "Then don't lose control."

"It's not that simple," Viktor snapped, frustration bubbling up inside him. He turned away from her, staring out over the city again. "You have no idea what you're asking."

"I know exactly what I'm asking," Lila said, stepping up beside him, her voice unwavering. "I'm asking you to trust me. To trust that we can figure this out together."

Viktor's hands clenched at his sides, his mind racing. He had lived for centuries, long enough to know that trust was a dangerous thing in his world. It was fragile, easily broken, and the consequences of betrayal could be deadly. But there was something about Lila—something in the way she looked at him, in the way she believed in him—that made him want to believe her.

But belief wasn't enough. Not when the stakes were this high.

"I don't know if I can do that," Viktor admitted, his voice barely above a whisper.

Lila's hand gently touched his arm, and the warmth of her skin sent a jolt through him. He stiffened but didn't pull away. Her touch was soft, grounding, and for a moment, Viktor allowed himself to savour the feeling of her presence, the calm she brought to the storm raging inside him.

"You can," Lila said quietly. "You already have."

He turned to face her, his dark eyes searching hers for something—anything—that would make this easier. But there was no easy way out of this. The Bloodbound bond between them was growing, deepening, and with it came the intense desire to protect her, to keep her safe at all costs. But there was something else too. Something more dangerous.

He wanted her. Not just as a protector, not just as someone bound by fate. He wanted her in ways he hadn't allowed himself to want anyone in centuries. And that was the most dangerous thing of all.

"I've crossed a line," Viktor said, his voice low and filled with regret. "And if I don't stop now, I won't be able to turn back."

Lila's eyes softened, and she stepped closer, her gaze never wavering. "Maybe I don't want you to turn back."

Viktor's heart ached at her words, torn between the overwhelming pull he felt toward her and the deep-seated knowledge that his world would ruin her if he let her in any further.

"You don't know what you're saying," Viktor said, his voice strained. "If we seal the bond, you'll lose everything. Your humanity, your life as you know it. You'll be drawn into a world of danger, of violence, of—"

"A world I'm already in," Lila interrupted, her voice firm. "I've been a part of your world since the night you saved me. And I'm not running from it."

Viktor's breath caught in his throat. The determination in her voice, the unwavering resolve in her eyes—it shook him to his core. She wasn't afraid, not of him, not of the bond, not of the danger that surrounded them. And that terrified him more than anything else.

"I don't deserve your trust," Viktor said, his voice barely above a whisper.

Lila smiled softly, her hand still resting on his arm. "Maybe not. But I'm giving it to you anyway."

For a long moment, they stood in silence, the tension between them thick and electric. Viktor could feel the pull of the bond, stronger than ever under the weight of the Blood Moon's fading influence. It would be so easy to close the distance between them, to give in to the desire that burned within him. But he knew that once he crossed that line, there would be no going back.

"I can't protect you if I lose control," Viktor said, his voice rough with emotion.

"Then don't lose control," Lila whispered, her eyes locked with his. "Let's figure this out together."

Viktor's resolve wavered, his heart torn between the need to protect her and the desire to be with her. He had spent centuries building walls around himself, shutting out any possibility of feeling this way. But Lila had broken through those walls with her courage, her kindness, her belief in him.

And now, standing on the edge of the precipice, Viktor knew that he was about to cross the line.

But this time, he wasn't sure he wanted to turn back.

With a heavy breath, Viktor stepped closer, his eyes never leaving hers. The air between them crackled with tension, and for the first time in centuries, Viktor allowed himself to hope—hope that maybe, just maybe, he could trust her.

And with that hope came a terrifying realization: he couldn't resist her any longer.

As Viktor leaned in, his lips inches from hers, the world around them seemed to fade away. There was only Lila, only the bond between them, only the forbidden attraction that had grown too powerful to deny.

But even as his heart raced and his pulse quickened, a dark voice in the back of his mind whispered a warning: once you cross this line, there's no going back.

And for the first time, Viktor wasn't sure he cared.

# Chapter 8: Seduction in Shadows

The night sky outside Lila's apartment was a blanket of stars, shimmering faintly against the inky darkness. But inside, the air was thick, charged with a tension neither she nor Viktor could ignore any longer. The pull between them had grown, a magnetic force that had been building for weeks, and now, standing inches apart in the dimly lit room, the bond they shared felt impossible to resist.

Viktor's eyes, dark and intense, searched Lila's face, as if he was fighting an internal battle he knew he was destined to lose. The quiet hum of the city outside faded away, leaving only the sound of their breathing—shallow, uneven—as they stood suspended in a moment that felt both inevitable and forbidden.

Lila's heart raced, her pulse quickening in anticipation. She could feel the heat of Viktor's body despite the cold aura that seemed to surround him, a reminder of what he was. Yet the fear she had once felt had been replaced by something else, something far more dangerous—desire.

She had been drawn to him since the moment they met, but now, standing so close, the desire she felt was overwhelming. She knew the risks, knew that falling for him could unravel her entire life, but the connection between them was undeniable. The Bloodbound bond had linked them in ways she hadn't anticipated, but it wasn't just the bond that made her want him.

It was him. Viktor. The brooding, tortured vampire who had saved her life and, in doing so, had somehow become a part of hers.

"You shouldn't be this close to me," Viktor said, his voice a low growl, barely more than a whisper. His gaze flickered with both longing and restraint, and Lila could see the battle raging behind his dark eyes. "You have no idea what you're inviting."

Lila's breath hitched, but she didn't move away. Instead, she stepped closer, her chest brushing against his. Her heart was pounding so loudly she was sure he could hear it. She didn't care. All the warnings, all the danger—they felt distant, insignificant compared to the fire burning inside her.

"I know exactly what I'm inviting," Lila whispered, her voice steady despite the tremble in her hands. "And I don't care."

Viktor closed his eyes for a moment, his jaw clenched as if he was trying to summon the strength to step back, to stop what was about to happen. But when he opened his eyes again, the control he had fought so hard to maintain seemed to slip. The intensity in his gaze deepened, filled with a hunger Lila had never seen before.

"You should care," Viktor murmured, his voice rough, as if he was barely holding on. "I've lived for centuries trying to avoid this."

"And now?" Lila asked, her voice barely audible as her fingers lightly brushed his arm.

Viktor's breath hitched at the contact, and he shook his head, though his actions betrayed his words. "Now... I don't know how to stop."

Lila's heart fluttered at his words. She knew this moment was dangerous, knew they were walking the edge of a cliff. But something inside her wanted to jump, wanted to take the risk, wanted to let go of the fear and embrace the desire that had been simmering between them.

Before she could think twice, Lila closed the final gap between them, her hand resting on his chest as she tilted her head up to meet his gaze. Viktor's eyes darkened with desire, his breath shallow as he stared down at her. The air between them felt thick, charged with a tension that threatened to consume them both.

And then, without warning, Viktor's resolve shattered.

He closed the distance between them in one swift motion, his lips crashing against hers with a passion that took Lila's breath away. The kiss was fierce, intense, as if Viktor had been holding back for too long and now, all the emotions he had kept locked away were pouring out in this one, desperate moment.

Lila melted into him, her arms wrapping around his neck as she pressed herself against him. His lips were cold, but his kiss ignited a fire inside her, one that spread through her veins like wildfire. She had never felt anything like it before—the sheer intensity of the connection between them, the way his touch made her skin tingle, her heart race.

Viktor's hands gripped her waist, pulling her closer as if he couldn't get enough, as if he needed her in a way that went beyond physical desire. The kiss deepened, their breaths mingling as the world around them seemed to disappear. There was no Vampire Council, no Crimson Shadows, no ancient curses—only the two of them, lost in a moment they had both been trying to avoid.

But as the kiss grew more urgent, more desperate, a flicker of something dark passed through Viktor's mind. His grip on her waist tightened, his body tensing as he pulled away, breaking the kiss with a ragged breath.

Lila's chest heaved, her mind spinning as she tried to process what had just happened. She had never felt anything so intense, so raw. But when she looked up at Viktor, she saw the torment in his eyes—the internal war he was fighting.

"We can't," Viktor said, his voice strained, as if each word cost him a piece of his soul. "I can't lose control like that."

Lila's breath caught, and she reached out to touch his arm, but he flinched away, stepping back as if he was afraid of what might happen if they touched again.

"This bond between us," Viktor continued, his voice low and filled with regret. "It's dangerous. I shouldn't have let it get this far."

"Viktor," Lila whispered, taking a step toward him, but he shook his head, his eyes dark with guilt.

"I don't want to hurt you, Lila," he said, his voice barely above a whisper. "But if we keep this up... if we seal this bond... I won't be able to stop myself."

Lila's chest tightened, her mind racing. She had known the bond was dangerous, but she hadn't expected Viktor to be this torn, this afraid of what might happen if they gave in to it.

"You won't hurt me," she said softly, though she wasn't sure she believed it.

Viktor's expression hardened, his jaw clenched. "You don't know that. I can feel the hunger growing stronger every time we're together. I'm not just a vampire, Lila—I'm a predator. And you're the one thing I can't afford to lose control over."

Lila's heart ached at the pain in his voice, the fear of what he might become if he let go. But she also knew that the bond between them was real, undeniable, and growing stronger by the day. And despite the danger, despite the risk, she wasn't ready to walk away.

"What if I don't care about the danger?" she asked, her voice trembling. "What if I want to take the risk?"

Viktor's eyes flashed with something dark, something primal, but he shook his head again, taking another step back. "It's not your decision to make, Lila. I won't let you lose yourself because of me."

Lila's breath hitched. She wanted to argue, to tell him that she could handle it, that the bond between them was worth the risk. But deep down, she knew that Viktor was right. This wasn't just about attraction or desire—it was about something far more dangerous.

"I don't want to hurt you," Viktor whispered, his voice filled with anguish. "But if we keep this up, I might."

Lila stood frozen, torn between the desire she felt for him and the fear of what might happen if they gave in to the bond completely. The kiss had ignited something between them—something neither of them could deny—but it had also brought them closer to a line neither was ready to cross.

Viktor took a deep breath, his eyes locking with hers one last time before he turned and walked toward the window.

"I need time," he said softly, his voice filled with regret. "Time to figure out how to protect you... from me."

And with that, he disappeared into the shadows, leaving Lila standing alone in the dimly lit room, her heart aching with the knowledge that the passion they had ignited might be the very thing that would destroy them both.

# Chapter 9: The Hunt Begins

The night was unnaturally quiet, as if the city itself was holding its breath. Lila stood at her window, staring out into the darkness, her mind still reeling from what had happened with Viktor. She could still feel the ghost of his kiss on her lips, the heat of his touch lingering on her skin. But it wasn't just the kiss that had left her unsettled—it was the warning in his eyes, the fear that he was losing control.

Her thoughts spiralled, filled with questions and uncertainty. How could something that felt so right be so dangerous? And what would happen if they couldn't resist the pull of the Bloodbound bond?

But tonight, the silence felt ominous, and her unease wasn't only about Viktor. Something else lurked in the shadows—something darker, more dangerous.

A knock at the door made Lila jump, her heart leaping into her throat. It was late—too late for visitors—and a creeping dread spread through her as she hesitated, listening for any sound outside. But there was only silence.

She slowly approached the door, her pulse quickening with every step. She reached for the handle, but before she could touch it, a voice whispered from the shadows behind her.

"Don't."

Lila spun around, her breath catching in her throat. Viktor stood in the corner of the room, his expression dark, his eyes filled with a mixture of urgency and fear. He moved toward her swiftly, his presence commanding, and without thinking, Lila took a step back.

"Viktor," she whispered, her heart pounding. "What's going on?"

His jaw tightened, his eyes flickering toward the door before returning to her. "They're here."

Lila's blood ran cold. "Who?"

"The Crimson Shadows," Viktor said quietly, his voice low and tense. "They've learned about us. They know about the bond."

Panic surged through her, and Lila's mind raced. The Crimson Shadows—Viktor had warned her about them before. A rival vampire clan, ruthless and relentless, known for their cruelty. And now they were after her.

Lila's breath quickened, and she took a step closer to Viktor. "What do they want with me?"

"They know about the Bloodbound," Viktor replied, his voice tight with barely concealed rage. "They want to use you as leverage against me. If they take you, they'll force my hand."

Lila's chest tightened. "Force your hand to do what?"

Viktor's eyes darkened, and for a moment, Lila saw a flicker of something raw in his expression. "The Crimson Shadows have been seeking power for centuries. If they control you, if they use our bond... they could control me."

Lila's pulse raced, the weight of his words sinking in. The bond between them wasn't just a connection of desire or attraction—it was something far more dangerous. Something that others could exploit.

"They're not here for you, Lila," Viktor said quietly, his voice barely more than a whisper. "They're here for us."

A cold chill swept through her, and Lila felt the weight of the danger pressing down on her. She had always known Viktor's world was dangerous, but this was something she hadn't fully understood. The Crimson Shadows weren't just enemies—they were predators, and she was their prey.

"What do we do?" she asked, her voice trembling.

Viktor's gaze shifted to the door, his expression grim. "We run."

Lila's heart pounded in her chest as she grabbed her coat, her mind spinning. "Where can we go?"

"There's a safe house outside the city," Viktor said, his voice steady despite the tension in the air. "A place where the Crimson Shadows can't reach us. We'll be safe there for now."

Lila nodded, her hands shaking as she gathered her things. She couldn't believe this was happening—couldn't believe that her life had taken such a dark turn. Only a few weeks ago, her biggest worry had been a late work deadline, and now she was running from vampires.

But there was no time to think, no time to process the fear that gnawed at her insides. Viktor was already at the door, listening intently for any movement outside. The silence was thick, suffocating, as if the world itself was waiting for something to break.

"They're close," Viktor muttered, his eyes narrowing. "We need to go. Now."

Lila's heart raced as she followed Viktor out the back door, her feet barely touching the ground as they moved through the dark alleyways of the city. Every shadow felt like a threat, every sound a warning. She glanced over her shoulder, but there was nothing—only the oppressive stillness of the night.

They moved quickly, Viktor's presence reassuring in its strength and precision. But even as they hurried through the deserted streets, Lila could feel the weight of the Crimson Shadows closing in. The air was thick with danger, the scent of something ancient and malevolent hanging over them like a storm cloud.

"Viktor," she whispered, her breath ragged as they darted around a corner. "How do they know about us?"

Viktor's jaw clenched, and for a moment, he didn't answer. When he finally spoke, his voice was low, filled with barely restrained fury. "There are spies everywhere in the vampire world. The moment I returned to your side, they must have sensed it. The Crimson Shadows have been waiting for an opportunity like this."

Lila's heart sank. It wasn't just about her—it was about Viktor. The rival clan wanted to use her to control him, to manipulate the bond they shared for their own gain. She was nothing more than a pawn in a game she barely understood.

Suddenly, a blur of movement flashed in the corner of Lila's vision. She barely had time to react before Viktor grabbed her arm, pulling her into the shadows of a nearby alleyway.

"Stay close," he hissed, his eyes scanning the darkness around them. "They're here."

Lila's breath caught in her throat as she pressed herself against the brick wall, her heart hammering in her chest. The night seemed to close in around them, the weight of unseen eyes watching from every corner. She could feel the presence of the Crimson Shadows—an oppressive, malevolent force that made her skin crawl.

Viktor's body was tense, his eyes glowing with the faintest hint of red as he listened for any sign of their pursuers. The air around him seemed to crackle with energy, a reminder of the power he held beneath his calm exterior.

And then, without warning, they attacked.

A figure darted out of the shadows, moving faster than Lila could comprehend. Viktor reacted in an instant, throwing himself between her and the attacker with a speed and strength that took her breath away. The two figures collided with a force that rattled the very air around them, and for a moment, all Lila could see was a blur of movement, a tangle of limbs as Viktor fought off the vampire who had come for them.

But it wasn't just one.

More figures emerged from the darkness, their eyes glowing with a feral hunger as they closed in on Lila and Viktor. The Crimson Shadows. They moved with terrifying speed, their movements graceful yet deadly as they circled their prey.

"Run!" Viktor growled, his voice filled with urgency as he deflected another blow from one of the attackers. "Go!"

Lila's feet felt frozen to the ground, fear rooting her in place as she watched Viktor fight off the vampires with an intensity that sent chills down her spine. But she knew she couldn't stay. If she did, she would only be a distraction, and Viktor wouldn't be able to protect them both.

With a shaky breath, Lila turned and ran, her heart pounding as she sprinted down the alleyway. The sound of the fight behind her echoed in her ears, the brutal clash of fists and fangs a reminder of just how dangerous this world truly was.

She didn't stop running until she reached the end of the alley, her lungs burning as she gasped for breath. But as she paused to catch her breath, a shadow loomed in front of her, blocking her path.

One of the Crimson Shadows.

The vampire grinned, his eyes gleaming with malice as he stepped toward her. Lila's heart raced, her mind scrambling for a way out, but before she could move, the vampire lunged.

And then, in a flash of movement too fast to see, Viktor was there.

He slammed into the vampire with a force that sent both of them crashing into the brick wall, the sound of the impact reverberating through the alley. Viktor's eyes glowed with a dangerous red light as he pinned the vampire to the wall, his voice a low growl.

"Stay away from her."

The vampire snarled, but Viktor didn't give him a chance to respond. With a swift, brutal motion, Viktor snapped the vampire's neck, and the body crumpled to the ground, lifeless.

Lila stood frozen, her heart racing as she stared at the scene in front of her. The danger wasn't over, but for the moment, they were safe.

Viktor turned to her, his eyes still glowing with the remnants of the fight, and for a moment, Lila saw the depth of the anger and fear that had been driving him.

"We need to go," Viktor said, his voice steady despite the tension in the air. "There will be more."

Lila nodded, her mind still reeling from the attack. She knew now that the Crimson Shadows wouldn't stop. They wanted her—and they wanted Viktor's power. And as long as their bond remained unsealed, they would stop at nothing to capture her.

As Viktor led her away, disappearing into the shadows once more, Lila realized that the hunt had only just begun.

# Chapter 10: Marked by Darkness

The moon hung high in the night sky, casting a pale glow over the deserted streets as Lila and Viktor fled through the shadows. The adrenaline from their encounter with the Crimson Shadows still coursed through Lila's veins, her heart pounding in her chest as they darted down another alley. The eerie silence of the city only heightened her sense of danger. She could feel the weight of something dark closing in on her, though she couldn't quite explain what it was.

Her legs burned from running, but the fear driving her forward overpowered the pain. Viktor was silent beside her, his expression tight, eyes scanning the streets for any sign of their enemies. They had escaped the initial attack, but Lila knew they weren't safe—not yet.

Suddenly, Viktor came to a stop, grabbing Lila's arm and pulling her into the deep shadows of an alleyway. His body pressed against hers as they hid, his breath steady despite the intensity of the chase. Lila's heart raced as she leaned against the cold brick wall, trying to catch her breath.

"They're gone... for now," Viktor murmured, his eyes still glowing faintly in the dark. "But we don't have much time."

Lila's breath came in shaky gasps as she nodded. She could feel the tension radiating from Viktor, the barely restrained anger from their encounter with the Crimson Shadows. But something else gnawed at her—a sense of unease that had nothing to do with the chase. Her skin felt... different. Tingles of coldness and an unfamiliar pressure clung to her, an odd sensation she couldn't shake.

"What happened back there?" Lila asked, her voice trembling as she clutched Viktor's arm. "I thought we got away, but... something feels wrong."

Viktor's eyes darkened, and he stepped back, scanning her as if searching for an answer he didn't want to find. His gaze landed on her arm, and his expression hardened. "Show me your arm."

Confused, Lila slowly lifted her sleeve, revealing her forearm. What she saw made her stomach churn.

A dark, swirling mark—black as night—curled across her skin like tendrils of smoke. It pulsed faintly, as if it were alive, and the sight of it sent a wave of nausea through her. The skin around the mark felt cold, almost as if it had been seared by ice.

"Viktor," Lila whispered, her voice shaking. "What... what is this?"

Viktor's face tightened, his jaw clenched in anger and frustration. He reached out, his fingers brushing the mark on her skin. The contact sent a shiver through Lila, the mark reacting to Viktor's touch as if it recognized him.

"They've marked you," Viktor said, his voice low, filled with a barely contained fury. "It's a curse. One meant to bind you to them."

Lila's heart skipped a beat. A curse? The word echoed in her mind, sending a jolt of fear through her. "What does that mean? What happens now?"

"It's a dark spell," Viktor explained, his voice tight. "The Crimson Shadows must have cast it during the attack. It links your fate to mine. They know about our bond, and they're trying to manipulate it, to control it. As long as that mark stays on you, you're vulnerable. They can track you, use the curse to get to me."

Lila's mind raced, panic bubbling up inside her. "Can we break it? How do we get rid of it?"

Viktor's expression darkened. "It's not that simple. This isn't an ordinary curse—it's ancient magic, tied to the Bloodbound bond between us. Breaking it would be dangerous. It could sever the bond or worse... it could harm you."

Lila's breath hitched. She stared at the mark on her arm, fear gnawing at her insides. She had always known her connection to Viktor was dangerous, but this—this was something far worse. Her fate, her life, was now bound to his in ways she couldn't control. The Crimson

Shadows had marked her as a tool to get to Viktor, and now they had power over her.

"What do we do?" she whispered, her voice trembling.

Viktor's eyes met hers, and for a moment, the anger melted away, replaced by something softer—something more vulnerable. "We protect you. I won't let them take you, Lila."

His words sent a shiver through her, but the fear gnawing at her heart didn't lessen. "How can we protect me if they can track me through this?"

Viktor glanced down at the mark again, his brow furrowed in thought. "There's a way to weaken the curse, at least temporarily. But it's dangerous. It involves magic—dark magic."

Lila's stomach twisted. Dark magic. The very idea of it made her feel sick, but the alternative—being hunted, being controlled by the Crimson Shadows—was worse.

"What do we need to do?" she asked, her voice barely above a whisper.

Viktor hesitated, his gaze flickering with uncertainty. "There's someone... an old ally of mine. She deals in magic, but her methods are unpredictable. If anyone can help us, it's her."

Lila nodded, trying to steady her nerves. She didn't have a choice. She couldn't go on like this, marked by darkness, her life hanging by a thread that the Crimson Shadows could pull at any moment.

"We'll go to her," Viktor said, his voice firm. "But you need to know—dealing with this kind of magic comes at a cost. It could make things worse."

Lila swallowed hard, fear and uncertainty clouding her thoughts. But as she looked into Viktor's eyes, she saw the determination there, the promise that he wouldn't let anything happen to her.

"I trust you," she said softly, her voice trembling but filled with resolve.

Viktor's expression softened for a brief moment before he nodded. "Then we leave now."

Without another word, Viktor led Lila through the dark streets, his grip on her arm firm but gentle, as if he feared she might slip away from him. Lila's thoughts raced as they moved quickly through the shadows, her mind spinning with the weight of what had just happened. The mark on her arm pulsed faintly, a constant reminder of the darkness that now tethered her to Viktor's world.

As they moved deeper into the night, Lila couldn't shake the feeling that this was only the beginning. The Crimson Shadows had marked her, and now her life was tied to Viktor's in a way that went beyond the Bloodbound bond. Her fate was no longer her own, and she had no idea what the future held.

All she knew was that the darkness was closing in, and the line between who she was and what she was becoming was growing thinner by the second.

# Chapter 11: The Bond Deepens

The dimly lit room was heavy with the weight of unspoken truths. Lila sat on the edge of the worn sofa in the old safe house Viktor had brought her to after their deadly encounter with the Crimson Shadows. The strange mark still pulsed faintly on her arm, a constant reminder of the curse now binding her to Viktor—and of the dark forces hunting them. But it wasn't just the curse that unsettled her; it was the deepening bond she felt with Viktor. It was as if something in her soul had shifted, something irreversible.

Viktor stood by the window, his tall frame silhouetted against the moonlight that streamed in through the cracks in the blinds. His face was unreadable, a mixture of tension and resolve etched into his features. He hadn't spoken much since they'd arrived, but Lila could feel the weight of the silence pressing down on them both. There was something he wasn't telling her—something he was holding back.

Finally, unable to take the silence any longer, Lila broke the stillness. "What aren't you telling me?"

Viktor didn't turn to face her, his gaze fixed on the shadows outside the window. For a moment, she wasn't sure he'd answer. But then, in a voice that was quieter than she had ever heard from him, he said, "There's something you need to understand about the Bloodbound."

Lila's heart skipped a beat. She had heard the term before, had felt its weight hanging over them since Viktor had first saved her life. But now, with everything that had happened—the mark, the curse, the undeniable pull she felt toward him—she knew there was more to the bond than she had realized.

"Tell me," she said softly, her voice steady despite the nerves tightening in her chest.

Viktor finally turned to face her, his dark eyes filled with an intensity that sent a shiver through her. He took a deep breath, as if he were preparing himself to reveal a truth that could change everything.

"The Bloodbound is more than just a connection," he began, his voice low and rough. "It's not just about attraction or desire. It's not just about power. It's... a binding of souls."

Lila blinked, her breath catching in her throat. "Souls?"

Viktor nodded, his gaze unwavering. "The moment we sealed the Bloodbound bond—when I saved your life and our connection began to form—our souls became linked. It's more than just a bond between a vampire and a human. It's deeper, stronger than that. It's eternal."

Lila's mind spun, trying to process what he was saying. Soul-bound. Eternal. The words echoed in her mind, heavy with meaning. This wasn't just some fleeting connection. This was something far more permanent, far more dangerous—and far more intimate.

"So... we're bound together," Lila said slowly, her voice barely above a whisper. "For life?"

"For life," Viktor confirmed, his eyes never leaving hers. "And beyond."

The weight of his words hit her like a tidal wave. The bond between them wasn't just powerful—it was forever. No matter what happened, no matter where life—or death—took them, their souls were tied together in ways she hadn't fully understood until now.

Lila swallowed hard, her mind racing with questions. "What does that mean for us? What happens now?"

Viktor hesitated, his expression clouded with a mixture of regret and longing. "It means that our connection will only grow stronger with time. You'll feel my presence even when I'm not near. You'll feel my emotions, my pain, my desires... just as I will feel yours."

Lila's heart pounded in her chest. She had already begun to sense that connection—the way her thoughts often drifted to Viktor even when he wasn't there, the way she could feel his tension and anger during the fight with the Crimson Shadows. But to hear him say it so plainly, to confirm that their souls were now intertwined, was overwhelming.

"And the curse?" she asked quietly, her gaze dropping to the dark mark still pulsing on her arm. "What does that mean for the bond?"

Viktor's jaw tightened, and for a moment, Lila thought he wouldn't answer. But then, in a voice filled with barely restrained anger, he said, "The Crimson Shadows know about the Bloodbound. They marked you because they know that if they control you, they control me."

Lila's breath hitched. "But I'm not... I'm not a vampire. How can they control me?"

"The Bloodbound bond ties us together," Viktor explained, his voice low and tense. "If they manipulate the curse, they can use it to exploit our connection. They can use the mark to weaken me, to control my actions. And if they gain control over you... they can force me to do whatever they want."

A cold shiver ran down Lila's spine. She had never asked for this, had never wanted to be part of Viktor's dark world. But now, it seemed, her fate was tied to his in ways she couldn't escape. The Crimson Shadows weren't just after Viktor—they were after her. And they were willing to use the bond between them to gain power.

"Is there any way to break it?" she asked, her voice trembling. "The curse, the bond... can we stop this?"

Viktor shook his head, his expression grim. "The Bloodbound bond is eternal. There's no way to break it—not without destroying both of us. As for the curse... it can be weakened, but it's dangerous. We'll need to go deeper into the dark magic that created it."

Lila's stomach churned at the thought. Dark magic. The very idea made her feel sick, but what choice did she have? She couldn't live like this, constantly hunted, constantly under threat. And she couldn't bear the thought of Viktor being controlled by the very bond that tied them together.

"What do we do?" she whispered, her voice barely audible.

Viktor stepped closer, his presence commanding and reassuring all at once. He knelt in front of her, his dark eyes filled with a mixture of determination and something softer—something that made her heart ache.

"We fight," he said quietly, his voice filled with resolve. "We fight the Crimson Shadows, we fight the curse, and we protect each other. I won't let them take you, Lila. I won't let them use you against me."

His words sent a shiver through her, and despite the fear gnawing at her insides, Lila felt a surge of warmth at his promise. She had never expected to be caught in a world of vampires, curses, and ancient magic, but now that she was, she knew one thing for certain: she wasn't alone.

Viktor was with her.

And together, they would face whatever darkness came their way.

But as she looked into his eyes, the full weight of the Bloodbound bond pressing down on her, Lila couldn't help but wonder what price they would both have to pay for their connection. The bond between them was deep, eternal—and it was growing stronger every day.

And with every deepening thread of that connection, the risks only grew.

Their souls were bound. Their fates intertwined.

But as the darkness closed in around them, Lila couldn't shake the feeling that the most dangerous part of all wasn't the curse, or the Crimson Shadows, or even the Bloodbound bond.

It was the way her heart had become irrevocably tied to Viktor's.

# Chapter 12: A Heart Divided

The days following Viktor's revelation were filled with an oppressive silence. Lila had always been independent, a person who could tackle anything on her own terms. But now, as the truth of her bond with Viktor sank in, she felt as though her entire life had spiralled out of her control. The knowledge that they were soul-bound—tied together for eternity—was both overwhelming and terrifying. The mark on her arm pulsed as a constant reminder of the darkness that had entwined itself with her fate.

Lila stood by the window of the safe house, staring out at the city. The sky was a dull grey, as though even the world outside was weighed down by the storm brewing in her mind. Her thoughts raced in circles, the same questions gnawing at her day and night.

Could she survive in Viktor's world? Could she live with the constant danger that came with being tied to a vampire, knowing that powerful enemies hunted her, using her as leverage to control him? Was love—if she could even call what she felt for him love—enough to keep her anchored in this nightmare?

Behind her, the sound of Viktor moving around the small room was a constant presence. He didn't speak much anymore, sensing the turmoil inside her, giving her space to sort through the tangled mess of emotions that had built up since their bond had deepened. Yet, his silence only seemed to intensify her inner conflict.

Lila's heart was torn in two. On one side, she felt the undeniable connection to Viktor—a pull that went beyond mere attraction, something raw and primal that had grown into something deeper. She trusted him, cared for him more than she had ever thought possible. But on the other side was fear—the fear of losing herself completely in a world of darkness, of vampires, curses, and ancient rivalries.

Could she really live like this? Constantly looking over her shoulder, hunted by the Crimson Shadows? Was it even possible for her to return to any semblance of a normal life?

"Lila," Viktor's voice interrupted her thoughts, soft but firm.

She turned to find him standing near the door, his dark eyes watching her with a mixture of concern and frustration. He had sensed her growing distance, and though he hadn't pressed her, she knew the time had come for her to confront the questions that had been tearing her apart.

"I can't do this," she blurted out, the words escaping her before she could stop them.

Viktor's expression didn't change, but she saw the flicker of pain behind his eyes. He stepped closer, his movements deliberate, but he stopped a few feet away, giving her the space she so desperately needed.

"What can't you do?" he asked, his voice calm despite the tension in the air.

Lila swallowed hard, her throat tight as the weight of her decision loomed before her. "I can't live in this world, Viktor. I'm not... I'm not like you. I'm not built for this."

His jaw clenched, and for a moment, Lila saw the conflict mirrored in his eyes. He had known this might happen, but that didn't make it any easier.

"I understand," he said quietly, though his voice was laced with pain. "This isn't the life you chose."

Lila shook her head, tears welling in her eyes. "I didn't ask for any of this—the bond, the curse, the danger. I'm not strong enough to survive here, Viktor. I'm not like you."

"You're stronger than you think," Viktor replied, his gaze never leaving hers. "You've already survived more than most could. You've faced the Crimson Shadows, fought off their attacks. You're stronger than you know, Lila."

"But at what cost?" Lila's voice cracked. "I'm losing myself. I can feel it. Every day, I'm pulled deeper into this world—your world—and I don't know if I can handle it. I don't even know if I want to."

Viktor's silence was heavy, and for a moment, the room seemed to close in around them, suffocating her. She had never been good at running away from things, but this—this was different. This was about survival, about keeping her soul intact. And yet, the thought of walking away from Viktor, of severing the connection between them, tore at her heart in ways she hadn't anticipated.

"You want to leave," Viktor said, his voice barely more than a whisper. "You think that's the answer."

"I don't know what the answer is," Lila admitted, her voice shaking. "But staying with you—it feels like I'm walking toward the edge of a cliff. And I'm terrified that one day, I'll fall, and there will be no coming back."

Viktor's expression darkened, a storm of emotions swirling behind his eyes. He took a step closer, his presence commanding and intense, but he didn't reach for her. He didn't try to hold her back. He simply stood there, watching her with a look of quiet desperation.

"I would never let you fall," he said softly, his voice thick with emotion. "I would protect you from anything, Lila. Even from myself."

Tears slipped down Lila's cheeks, and she wiped them away quickly, hating how vulnerable she felt. "But you can't protect me from this. From what's happening between us. The bond, the curse, everything—it's too much."

Viktor closed his eyes for a moment, as if trying to regain control of the emotions that threatened to spill over. When he opened them again, his gaze was filled with a sorrow that broke Lila's heart.

"If you leave, the bond will remain," he said quietly. "You'll always feel it. No matter where you go, no matter how far you run, we'll always be connected. You won't escape that."

Lila's chest tightened at his words. Deep down, she knew he was right. The Bloodbound bond wasn't something she could just walk away from. It was a part of her now, a part of her soul. But could she live with that? Could she live with the constant reminder of what she had left behind?

"I don't know if I can do this," she whispered, her voice breaking. "I don't know if I'm strong enough to stay."

Viktor stepped closer, and this time, he reached for her hand, his touch gentle despite the turmoil raging between them. "You don't have to be strong alone. We can face this together. But whatever you decide, I won't hold you back. If leaving is what you need to do, I'll let you go."

Lila's heart ached at his words. She had expected him to argue, to try to convince her to stay. But instead, Viktor's willingness to let her go only made the decision that much harder. He was offering her freedom, even if it meant breaking his own heart.

Tears welled in her eyes as she looked up at him, her mind spinning. She had never felt so conflicted, so torn between two worlds. One world—the one she had known before—was safe, familiar. But it was also empty, devoid of the connection she now shared with Viktor. The other world—his world—was dangerous, filled with darkness and uncertainty. But it was also where her heart had led her.

"I don't want to lose you," she whispered, her voice barely audible. "But I don't know if I can survive this."

Viktor's grip on her hand tightened, and he pulled her closer, his eyes locking with hers. "Then stay. Stay, and we'll figure it out. Together."

Lila's heart raced, her thoughts tangled in a web of fear and desire. She wanted to stay, wanted to be with Viktor more than anything. But she couldn't ignore the voice in her head that warned her of the dangers that came with his world.

For a long moment, she stood there, torn between two impossible choices.

And in that moment, Lila realized that no matter what she decided, a part of her heart would always be divided.

# Chapter 13: The Council's Wrath

The air in the safe house was thick with tension, as if the walls themselves were holding their breath, waiting for something to shatter the fragile silence. Lila had barely slept in the days since she had confronted Viktor about her doubts. Though her heart had pulled her closer to him, the weight of their bond—and the dangers it carried—hung over her like a dark cloud.

But now, something far worse loomed on the horizon.

Viktor had become distant, more so than usual. Lila could sense the strain in his every movement, the way he avoided her gaze when he thought she wasn't looking. He was hiding something, and whatever it was, it made her stomach twist with dread. She could feel his unease through the bond they shared, a deep, unspoken tension that neither of them could ignore.

It wasn't long before her fears were confirmed.

Late one night, as Lila sat alone by the window, staring out into the darkened streets, Viktor finally spoke. His voice was low, heavy with the weight of something she hadn't heard in him before—fear.

"They know."

Lila turned to face him, her heart skipping a beat at the look in his eyes. He stood by the door, his posture rigid, his face a mask of controlled anger. But beneath it, she could see the flicker of something darker. The Vampire Council.

"Who knows?" she asked, though she already had a sinking feeling she knew the answer.

"The Council," Viktor said, his voice barely above a whisper. "They've discovered our bond."

Lila's stomach churned. She had heard about the Vampire Council from Viktor before, the shadowy governing body that ruled over all vampire clans with an iron fist. They enforced the laws that kept the vampire world in check, laws that Viktor had already broken by abandoning his clan years ago. But now, their relationship—their Bloodbound bond—had caught the Council's attention. And that was something they would not tolerate.

"What does that mean?" Lila asked, her voice trembling. "What are they going to do?"

Viktor clenched his fists at his sides, his jaw tight with frustration. "The Council considers any relationship between vampires and humans a threat. And the Bloodbound bond... it's forbidden. They believe it gives humans too much power, makes us vulnerable."

Lila's heart pounded in her chest as the weight of his words sank in. The Council saw her as a threat—not just because she was human, but because of the bond she shared with Viktor. A bond that, in their eyes, made him weaker. Vulnerable.

"They'll try to separate us," Viktor continued, his voice filled with quiet fury. "They've given me a choice—end the bond or face the consequences."

Lila's breath caught in her throat. "What consequences?"

Viktor's eyes darkened, and when he spoke again, his voice was laced with a barely contained anger. "If we don't end the bond, they'll come for us. They'll use whatever means necessary to break it, even if it means..." He trailed off, but Lila didn't need him to finish the sentence to understand the threat.

The Council wasn't just interested in ending their relationship. They would go as far as it took to sever the bond—even if that meant destroying both of them in the process.

Lila's pulse raced, her mind spinning with the implications. "So what do we do?"

Viktor took a deep breath, his eyes locking with hers. "We run."

Lila's heart ached at the desperation in his voice. She knew he was serious, that the Council's wrath was something far more dangerous than anything they had faced before. The Crimson Shadows were a threat, yes, but the Council... they were untouchable. Their reach extended far beyond the vampire clans. If they wanted Viktor and Lila gone, there would be nowhere to hide.

"Running won't stop them," Lila whispered, her voice thick with fear. "They'll find us eventually."

"I know," Viktor admitted, his eyes filled with a mixture of anger and regret. "But it will buy us time. Time to figure out a way to break the curse, to weaken the bond enough that they might leave us alone."

Lila shook her head, her thoughts racing. "But breaking the bond... it could destroy us both."

Viktor's jaw tightened, and for a moment, his control slipped, revealing the depth of his fear. "I know. But if we don't try... the Council will do far worse."

Lila's chest tightened with a painful mixture of fear and sadness. They had been running from danger since the moment their bond had formed, but this—this felt different. The Council was an unstoppable force, and now they were caught in its sights. Could they really survive this?

"Why do they care so much about us?" Lila asked, her voice trembling. "Why does the Bloodbound bond matter to them?"

Viktor's eyes darkened, and he took a step closer, his presence filling the small space between them. "The Council fears the power of the Bloodbound. They know that when a human and vampire are bonded, they become stronger together—stronger than any vampire alone. They see it as a threat to their control. And they fear what we might become."

Lila's heart raced as she processed his words. The Council wasn't just trying to end their relationship out of cruelty—they were afraid of what she and Viktor could become. The power of their bond was something they couldn't control, something that could disrupt the balance of power in the vampire world.

"But we haven't done anything," Lila protested, her voice cracking with emotion. "We're not trying to challenge them. We just..."

"We exist," Viktor finished, his voice filled with quiet fury. "And that's enough for them to see us as a threat."

Lila swallowed hard, her mind racing. She couldn't imagine a life without Viktor, couldn't imagine severing the bond between them. But if they didn't, if they defied the Council's orders, the consequences could be catastrophic. They would be hunted, pursued until there was nowhere left to run.

"Is there any other way?" she asked, her voice small. "Any way to convince them to let us be?"

Viktor's eyes softened, and for the first time in days, he reached out to her, gently brushing a strand of hair away from her face. "I wish there was. But the Council doesn't negotiate. They won't stop until the bond is broken."

Lila's heart ached at the tender touch, at the sadness in Viktor's eyes. She could feel his turmoil through the bond, the war raging inside him as he tried to figure out how to protect her, how to keep her safe from a world that wanted to tear them apart.

"I don't want to lose you," she whispered, tears welling in her eyes.

"You won't," Viktor said softly, his voice filled with both pain and determination. "We'll find a way. But first, we have to leave. We have to stay ahead of them."

Lila nodded, though her heart was heavy with the knowledge that their time was running out. The Council's wrath was coming for them, and there was no way to stop it. All they could do was run, hope that somehow, somewhere, they could find a way to weaken the bond without destroying themselves in the process.

But as Viktor pulled her into his arms, holding her close as if she might slip away at any moment, Lila couldn't shake the feeling that their love was being torn apart by forces far beyond their control. The bond between them was stronger than ever, but it was also the very thing that might destroy them.

And now, with the Council hunting them down, Lila knew that the fight for their survival had only just begun.

# Chapter 14: Between Love and Duty

The moon hung low in the night sky, casting an eerie glow over the darkened streets as Viktor and Lila hurried through the shadows. They had been running for hours, moving from safe house to safe house, trying to stay one step ahead of the Vampire Council. But with each passing moment, the weight of what was to come pressed harder on Viktor's shoulders.

For centuries, he had been a part of the vampire world, governed by its rules, its traditions. But now, for the first time in his long existence, those loyalties were being tested in ways he had never imagined. He had always been the dutiful vampire, loyal to the laws that kept their kind hidden and in control. But now, standing at the edge of everything he had known, Viktor found himself questioning it all.

The woman beside him, Lila, was everything to him. Their bond—Bloodbound, soul-bound—was unlike anything he had ever experienced, and the thought of losing her was unbearable. Yet, his heart was torn between two worlds: the one he had always known, bound by duty to the Council, and the one he was beginning to forge with Lila, built on love, danger, and defiance.

They slipped into another alleyway, Viktor's senses heightened as he scanned the surroundings for any sign of danger. He could feel Lila's unease through their bond, the way her thoughts flickered between fear and hope. It mirrored his own struggle.

"We can't keep running forever," Lila said, her voice a whisper in the night. "They're going to find us, aren't they?"

Viktor paused, turning to face her. Her face was pale in the moonlight, her eyes filled with both exhaustion and fear. But beneath the fear was something else—trust. She trusted him, even now, in the face of everything that threatened to tear them apart. That trust was a weight on Viktor's soul.

"They will find us," Viktor admitted quietly, his voice heavy. "The Council is relentless. But I won't let them take you, Lila. Not as long as I'm breathing."

Lila's eyes softened at his words, but he could sense the worry gnawing at her. "And what about you? What happens to you if you defy them?"

Viktor hesitated, the answer he had been avoiding now crashing down on him. Defying the Council meant betraying everything he had ever stood for. It meant becoming a target himself, hunted not just for the bond he had with Lila, but for the act of rebellion against the very laws that had governed his kind for centuries.

"The Council doesn't show mercy," Viktor said, his voice tight with anger. "If I defy them, they'll come for me, too. They'll consider me a traitor."

Lila's breath hitched, and Viktor could feel the surge of fear in her pulse. "So... what do we do? You can't fight them alone."

"I'm not alone," Viktor said, his gaze locking with hers. "I have you."

The words hung between them, filled with both promise and dread. Viktor knew what he had to do—he had already made his decision, deep in his heart. But saying it aloud, voicing it to Lila, made it feel all the more real. His loyalty to the vampire world, the world he had been a part of for centuries, was being tested in the most profound way. But his love for Lila outweighed everything else.

"I'm going to protect you, no matter the cost," Viktor said, his voice filled with quiet determination. "But I need you to understand something, Lila. The choice I'm making... it means turning my back on everything I've known. It means defying the Council, defying the laws that have governed me for centuries. Once I do this, there's no going back."

Lila's eyes widened as she took in the weight of his words. "You're going to choose me over them?"

Viktor's jaw tightened, the conflict within him still fresh, but the answer was clear in his heart. "I've already chosen you."

The admission sent a rush of warmth through Lila, but Viktor could sense the turmoil within her, the fear of what that choice might mean. He had defied his clan before, walking away from the life he had once known. But this was different. This was defiance on a scale that could end in both of their deaths.

"We can't just run forever, Viktor," Lila whispered, her voice trembling. "You said it yourself—they'll find us. What happens when they do?"

Viktor's gaze darkened. "When they find us, I'll fight. But the Council is powerful, and there's no guarantee we'll survive. That's why we need to figure out a way to weaken the bond, to sever the curse without destroying us in the process."

Lila's breath caught. She knew what that meant—what weakening the bond would entail. It would mean stepping back, letting go of the deeper connection between them, the one that had been growing stronger with each passing day. It would mean giving up the very thing that had tied them together in the first place.

"But if we weaken the bond, what does that mean for us?" Lila asked, her voice barely audible. "What happens to us?"

Viktor looked at her, his heart heavy with the truth he didn't want to face. "It means we might survive. But it also means that the connection we have... it won't be the same."

Lila's chest tightened with the weight of his words. The bond they shared—the Bloodbound, the tie that had bound their souls—was more than just a link between them. It was the very thing that had brought them together, that had deepened their feelings for one another. And now, they were faced with the possibility of losing it.

"I don't want to lose this," Lila whispered, her voice thick with emotion. "I don't want to lose you."

Viktor's heart ached at the pain in her voice, and he stepped closer, his hand gently cupping her face. "You won't lose me, Lila. No matter what happens, I'll always be with you. But we have to survive first. We have to make sure they can't use the bond against us."

Tears welled in Lila's eyes, and she leaned into his touch, her heart torn between love and fear. She didn't want to weaken the bond, didn't want to let go of the connection that had grown so powerful between them. But she knew Viktor was right. If they didn't do something, the Council would tear them apart.

"And what about your duty?" Lila asked softly, her eyes searching his. "What about your loyalty to the vampire world? Can you really leave it behind for me?"

Viktor's gaze darkened, his voice filled with quiet resolve. "My loyalty has always been to the vampire world, to the laws that govern us. But that world is broken, Lila. The Council rules with fear, and they'll destroy anyone who threatens their control. I've spent centuries obeying them, following their rules, but I can't do it anymore. Not if it means losing you."

Lila's heart raced at his words, the depth of his love for her clear in every word, every glance. He was willing to give up everything—his life, his loyalty, his world—for her. But at what cost? Could they really survive against a force as powerful as the Council?

"I love you," Viktor said quietly, his voice thick with emotion. "And I will fight for you, no matter the cost. But we have to make a choice now. We either weaken the bond and run, or we stand and face the Council, together."

Lila's breath hitched, her heart pounding in her chest. The choice before them was impossible, and no matter what they decided, there would be consequences. But as she looked into Viktor's eyes, filled with love and determination, she knew that her heart had already made its choice.

"We'll face them," she whispered, her voice steady despite the fear. "Together."

Viktor's expression softened, and he pulled her into his arms, holding her close as the weight of their decision settled over them. They would face the Council, defy the rules that had governed his life for centuries, and fight for their love.

But as the night closed in around them, Lila couldn't help but wonder what price they would have to pay for choosing love over duty.

# Chapter 15: Blood of Betrayal

The morning light filtered through the small window of the safe house, casting a soft glow over the room. For a brief moment, Lila allowed herself to imagine that life was normal again—that she wasn't being hunted, that the Vampire Council wasn't trying to tear her and Viktor apart, that her world hadn't been turned upside down by the bond she shared with him. But the weight of reality settled over her like a heavy cloak, and she knew the dangers they faced were far from over.

It had been a week since Viktor had told her about the Council's wrath, and every night since, Lila had found herself caught between fear and hope. Their decision to stand and fight together had filled her with determination, but the uncertainty of what lay ahead gnawed at her. They had been careful, staying off the radar, moving from safe house to safe house to avoid being tracked. But the constant hiding was taking its toll, both on her and on Viktor.

And then there was Emma.

Lila hadn't spoken to her best friend in days—not since everything had spiralled out of control. She missed her, missed the normalcy that Emma represented, but how could she explain any of this? How could she tell her best friend that she was caught up in a war between vampire clans, hunted by the most powerful vampire council in existence, and that she was bound—body and soul—to a vampire?

She couldn't. And the guilt of it weighed heavily on her.

But Emma had been texting her, asking questions that Lila didn't have answers for. At first, Lila had kept her replies vague, trying to protect her from the truth. But Emma was persistent, and Lila knew she couldn't keep her in the dark forever.

Lila was still sitting at the kitchen table, staring blankly at her phone, when Viktor returned from his latest scouting trip. He moved with his usual silent grace, his presence instantly commanding as he crossed the room to stand beside her.

"We're clear for now," Viktor said, his voice low, though there was a tension in his words. "No sign of the Council's enforcers."

Lila nodded, her heart heavy with the weight of their situation. "That's good," she said softly, though her mind was elsewhere.

Viktor frowned, sensing her distraction. He sat down across from her, his dark eyes searching hers. "Something's bothering you."

Lila sighed, running a hand through her hair. "It's Emma. She keeps texting me, and I don't know how to keep dodging her questions. She knows something's wrong, Viktor. I've never been this distant with her before."

Viktor's expression darkened. He had always been cautious about Lila's connection to the outside world, especially when it came to people who could unknowingly put them both in danger.

"Do you think she suspects anything?" he asked, his voice filled with concern.

Lila shook her head. "I don't know. I haven't told her anything, but she's my best friend. She knows me too well to believe everything's fine. I don't want to drag her into this mess, but I also hate lying to her."

Viktor's jaw tightened, and he leaned forward, his gaze serious. "Lila, if she finds out the truth, it could put her in danger—just like it has with you. The Council and the Crimson Shadows will stop at nothing to get to us. Anyone you're close to could become a target."

Lila's heart sank. She knew he was right, but that didn't make it any easier. Emma was her best friend, the one person who had been there for her through everything. The thought of keeping her in the dark felt like a betrayal in itself.

"I know," Lila whispered. "But it feels wrong."

Viktor reached out, gently taking her hand in his. "I'm not saying you should cut her off. But right now, you need to be careful. If you trust her, maybe you can find a way to explain enough without putting her at risk."

Lila nodded, though the knot of guilt in her stomach remained. She hated the secrecy, hated that her life had become something so dark and dangerous that she couldn't even confide in the person she trusted most. But what choice did she have?

As she sat there, her phone buzzed on the table, and Lila's heart skipped a beat when she saw Emma's name flash across the screen.

Emma: Hey, can we talk? I'm really worried about you.

Lila stared at the message, her fingers hovering over the screen. She hesitated, unsure of what to say. Before she could respond, Viktor stood and moved toward the window, his senses alert.

"I'll be outside, keeping watch," he said quietly, giving her space to deal with the situation in her own way.

Lila watched him go, her heart heavy with the weight of the secrets she was keeping. She took a deep breath and typed a quick reply to Emma, deciding it was time to at least tell her friend something.

Lila: I'm okay. Can we meet later? I can explain everything.

The message sent, and Lila felt a pang of anxiety wash over her. She couldn't tell Emma the full truth, but maybe she could find a way to ease her friend's worries without putting her in harm's way.

A few hours later, Lila made her way to the café where she and Emma had always met. It was a familiar place, one that used to feel comforting. But today, Lila felt uneasy, her nerves on edge as she waited at the back corner table, hidden from view. Viktor had insisted on watching from a distance, ensuring her safety without drawing attention.

Emma arrived right on time, her face a mixture of concern and relief as she spotted Lila. She rushed over, sitting down across from her with a worried expression.

"You're alive," Emma said, half-joking but clearly worried. "I've been losing my mind, Lila. What's going on?"

Lila sighed, wishing she could be as open as she used to be. "I'm sorry I've been so distant. There's... a lot going on."

"Clearly," Emma said, raising an eyebrow. "You vanish for days, you barely reply to my texts, and when you do, it's super vague. I know something's wrong. You can tell me, Lila. I'm here for you."

Lila swallowed hard. She had rehearsed what she would say on the way here, but now that she was sitting in front of Emma, the words felt heavy, difficult to release.

"There's... someone," Lila began slowly. "I've been involved with someone, and things are complicated. Dangerous, even."

Emma's eyes widened. "Dangerous? Lila, what do you mean? Is this guy—whoever he is—hurting you? Because if he is—"

"No, no," Lila said quickly, shaking her head. "It's not like that. He's... he's trying to protect me. But there are things—people—after us. That's why I've been distant."

Emma looked confused and sceptical. "After you? Lila, what are you talking about? This sounds like some kind of crime movie."

Lila struggled to find the right words, knowing how ridiculous it all sounded. But she couldn't tell her friend the full truth—not yet. "It's... complicated, Emma. I can't explain everything right now, but I promise I'm okay. I just need you to trust me."

Emma's eyes softened with concern, but she still seemed unsure. "I do trust you. I just don't want you getting hurt."

Lila smiled weakly. "I know. I'm trying to stay safe."

They talked for a while longer, and though Emma was clearly worried, she didn't press Lila too hard. As they said their goodbyes, Lila felt a strange sense of relief. Maybe she had managed to ease Emma's fears, if only for a little while.

But as Lila left the café and started walking back toward the safe house, something felt off. The streets seemed quieter than usual, and the hair on the back of her neck stood on end, as if someone was watching her. She quickened her pace, glancing over her shoulder, but saw nothing.

Suddenly, her phone buzzed, and when she pulled it out, her heart sank.

Emma: I'm sorry.

Before Lila could process what that meant, a figure appeared in front of her, emerging from the shadows. Lila gasped, stumbling backward, her pulse racing.

It was a vampire—one she didn't recognize. His eyes glowed with malevolent intent, and behind him, more figures emerged, surrounding her.

"You've been betrayed," the vampire hissed, a cruel smile spreading across his face. "Your friend led us right to you."

Lila's heart dropped as the realization hit her. Emma had unknowingly betrayed her—her concern for Lila had led her to confide in someone who was working with the Crimson Shadows. And now, Lila was trapped.

"Viktor!" she screamed, hoping he was close enough to hear.

But before she could react, the vampires lunged, and the world around her descended into chaos.

# Chapter 16: Shadows in the Heart

The aftermath of the ambush left Lila shaken to her core. Viktor had arrived just in time to fend off the vampires, but the damage had already been done. The betrayal by Emma—her best friend, the one person she had always trusted—cut deeper than any physical wound. Lila had known that the dangers of Viktor's world were real, but now, after nearly losing her life in the alley, the reality of those dangers felt suffocating.

The days that followed were a blur. Viktor kept her close, moving them to yet another safe house, but the weight of everything that had happened pressed down on her. Lila hadn't spoken to Emma since that night, and though Viktor assured her it wasn't Emma's fault—that she had likely been manipulated into revealing Lila's location—Lila couldn't shake the hollow ache of betrayal in her chest.

But that wasn't the only thing haunting her.

It was the shadows. The darkness that seemed to have crept into her life the moment she had met Viktor. Once, her world had been simple, full of light and normalcy. Now, everything had changed. She was bound to a vampire, hunted by the Vampire Council and rival clans, and cursed with a mark that made her a target. And despite everything, she had feelings for Viktor that ran deeper than anything she had ever known.

But love in Viktor's world was dangerous—lethal even. The attack had reminded her of that in the most brutal way. Her life, which had once been her own, now hung by a thread that could be severed at any moment. Every breath, every heartbeat, was tied to Viktor, and with him came the weight of the vampire world's darkest secrets.

It was too much to bear.

Lila sat in the quiet of the new safe house, staring out the window as the rain pattered softly against the glass. The city below was bathed in grey, reflecting the turmoil inside her. She hadn't seen Viktor all morning; he had left early, scouting the area for any sign of the Crimson Shadows or the Council's enforcers. But even in his absence, she could feel him—feel the bond that tied them together, the constant pull toward him that never let her go.

And that was what terrified her the most.

Love wasn't supposed to feel like this, wasn't supposed to be wrapped in shadows and danger. She was caught in a web of darkness that seemed to be pulling her deeper with every passing day, and the more she tried to hold on to who she was, the more it slipped away.

Could she keep doing this? Could she live in Viktor's world, knowing that at any moment, she could lose everything?

The door to the safe house creaked open, and Lila turned to see Viktor step inside, his presence immediately filling the room. He moved with the quiet grace of a predator, his eyes scanning the space as if checking for threats even here. When his gaze finally landed on her, there was a flicker of concern in his dark eyes.

"You've been quiet," he said, his voice soft but filled with the weight of everything unsaid.

Lila looked away, unable to meet his gaze. "I'm just... thinking."

Viktor crossed the room, sitting down beside her, his hand reaching out to gently touch her arm. "About what?"

Lila swallowed hard, her mind racing with the questions she had been avoiding for days. She knew she couldn't keep running from the truth—from the reality of what her life had become. She had to confront it, even if it meant making the hardest decision she had ever faced.

"About us," she whispered, her voice barely audible.

Viktor's hand stilled on her arm, and she could feel the tension in his body. "What about us?"

Lila took a deep breath, her heart pounding in her chest. "I don't know if I can do this, Viktor. I don't know if I can live in your world."

His eyes darkened, and though he didn't speak right away, she could sense the storm of emotions raging beneath his calm exterior. "You're not alone, Lila. You have me. We'll face this together."

"But that's just it," Lila said, her voice trembling. "Being with you means I'll never be free. I'll always be hunted, always be looking over my shoulder, waiting for the next attack. It's not just about the Council or the Crimson Shadows—it's about the darkness that comes with your world. The danger. The death."

Viktor's expression hardened, but there was a flicker of pain in his eyes. "I know this isn't easy. I've seen what it's done to you, and if I could take it all away, I would. But I can't change what I am, Lila. This is my world."

"And I'm not sure if it's mine," Lila whispered, her voice breaking.

The silence between them was heavy, filled with all the things neither of them wanted to say but both knew were true. Lila's heart ached as she looked at Viktor, the man she had grown to care for more deeply than anyone before. She didn't want to leave him, didn't want to sever the bond that had tied them together in ways she couldn't explain.

But she also knew that staying meant embracing the darkness. It meant accepting the fact that she would always be in danger, always at the mercy of forces far beyond her control.

"I can't ask you to stay," Viktor said softly, his voice thick with emotion. "I won't force you to live like this."

Lila's throat tightened. She could feel the love he had for her, the quiet desperation behind his words. But that only made the choice harder. She had thought she was strong enough to handle this, but the constant danger, the fear of losing everything, was wearing her down.

"I don't know what to do," she admitted, her voice barely a whisper.

Viktor reached out, gently cupping her face in his hands. His touch was cold, but comforting, and Lila leaned into it, closing her eyes as tears slipped down her cheeks.

"You don't have to decide right now," he said softly. "I'll be here, no matter what you choose."

Lila opened her eyes, meeting his gaze. "And if I decide to leave?"

Viktor's jaw tightened, but he didn't pull away. "Then I'll let you go."

The words hit her like a punch to the gut, and for a moment, Lila couldn't breathe. She had expected him to fight, to try to convince her to stay. But instead, he was offering her the one thing she hadn't expected: freedom.

But freedom came with a price.

Lila's heart raced as she looked into Viktor's eyes, torn between the love she felt for him and the fear of what staying by his side would mean. The shadows that had crept into her life weren't just a part of his world—they were now a part of her. And if she stayed, she knew she would have to embrace them fully.

The thought of leaving him tore at her, but so did the thought of losing herself completely in the darkness.

"I need time," Lila whispered, her voice thick with emotion. "I need to figure out if I can live like this."

Viktor nodded, though the pain in his eyes was unmistakable. "Take all the time you need."

Lila closed her eyes, leaning into his touch one last time, knowing that whatever decision she made, there would be no turning back.

She was caught between two worlds—one of light, one of darkness—and no matter which path she chose, she knew that love in Viktor's world would always come with deadly consequences.

# Chapter 17: A Taste of Immortality

The air in the safe house was thick with tension, the kind that seemed to weigh down on Lila with every breath she took. Days had passed since she'd admitted her doubts to Viktor, days filled with long stretches of silence punctuated by moments of deep conversation. Neither of them had spoken openly about the possibility of her leaving again, but the thought lingered between them, unspoken yet undeniable.

Lila stood by the window, staring out into the darkness, her mind a storm of thoughts she couldn't quiet. She could feel Viktor's presence behind her—he didn't need to say anything for her to know he was there, watching her with that quiet intensity he always carried. The bond between them hummed faintly, a constant reminder of the connection they shared, one that was growing harder to ignore with each passing day.

But tonight, something was different. There was an unspoken weight in the air, something beyond the usual tension of their situation. Viktor hadn't left for his usual scouting trips, and his silence had taken on a new kind of heaviness.

Finally, after what felt like hours, Viktor spoke.

"Lila," he said softly, his voice barely more than a whisper in the quiet room.

She turned slowly to face him, her heart pounding in her chest at the serious look in his eyes. He stood near the edge of the room, his tall, commanding presence almost filling the small space. His dark eyes were filled with something she couldn't quite place—an intensity that made her stomach twist with both fear and longing.

"I've been thinking," Viktor began, stepping closer, "about everything. About us, about the danger you're in because of me."

Lila swallowed hard, her heart racing. She had known this conversation was coming, but the reality of it still sent a chill down her spine.

"I don't want to lose you," Viktor continued, his voice thick with emotion. "But I also can't ignore the fact that as long as you remain human, you'll always be vulnerable. The Council, the Crimson Shadows... they'll never stop hunting us. And you'll always be at risk."

Lila's throat tightened, her mind racing as she tried to anticipate where this was going. She could feel the weight of his words, the importance of what he was about to say.

Viktor took another step closer, his gaze locking with hers. "There's another option. One I haven't offered before... because I didn't want to force it on you. But you deserve to know that it's a choice."

Lila's breath caught in her throat, and her pulse quickened. "What... what choice?"

Viktor's expression was solemn, and when he spoke, his voice was laced with both longing and hesitation. "You could become like me."

The words hung in the air, heavy and full of meaning.

Lila stared at him, her heart pounding in her chest as the weight of what he was offering crashed down on her. Become like him. Become a vampire. Immortal, bound by blood, living in the shadows of his world forever.

It was everything she had feared and everything she had tried to avoid thinking about since their bond had formed. The idea of giving up her humanity, of becoming something else entirely, sent a wave of fear and uncertainty through her.

"You're offering to turn me," Lila whispered, her voice trembling.

Viktor nodded, his eyes filled with both sadness and hope. "If you become like me, you won't be vulnerable anymore. The Council wouldn't be able to use you as leverage, and the Crimson Shadows wouldn't be able to exploit the bond between us. You'd be stronger, faster. You'd be... safe."

Safe. The word echoed in Lila's mind, but it didn't bring the comfort she had hoped for. Instead, it filled her with a sense of dread. Safety came at a price—her humanity.

"I don't know if I can do that," Lila said softly, her voice barely above a whisper. "I don't know if I want to be like you."

Viktor's jaw clenched, and for a moment, she saw the flicker of pain in his eyes. "I understand. It's not something I ever wanted to ask of you. But... if we're going to be together, if you're going to stay in my world, it's a choice you'll have to make eventually. Being human in my world... it's dangerous. It's deadly."

Lila turned away, her mind spinning with the enormity of the decision before her. The thought of living forever, of becoming a vampire, was both terrifying and exhilarating. She had spent her whole life as a human, bound by the limitations of time, of mortality. Becoming like Viktor would change everything—it would mean giving up the life she had known, the future she had imagined for herself.

But it would also mean she could stay with him. Stay with the man she had grown to love, the man who had risked everything to protect her. The bond between them would grow stronger, deeper, and they would never have to worry about the fragility of her human life.

But was that enough? Was love enough to make her give up her humanity, to step into a world of darkness and blood?

"I don't know if I can do this," Lila whispered, her voice breaking as tears welled in her eyes. "I don't know if I can live forever, like you. I don't know if I can give up who I am."

Viktor was silent for a long moment, and when he finally spoke, his voice was filled with both understanding and sorrow. "I won't force you. I would never force you, Lila. But I need you to know that this world... it's not kind to humans. It's cruel. And as long as you're human, you'll always be in danger."

Lila's heart ached at the truth in his words. She knew he was right. She had already seen the darkness of Viktor's world—the violence, the bloodshed, the constant threat of death. Staying human meant living with that danger every day, never knowing if the next attack would be her last.

But becoming a vampire... it felt like losing herself.

"I don't want to lose you," Viktor said quietly, his voice filled with emotion. "But I don't want you to feel like you have to make this choice for me."

Lila wiped away the tears that had slipped down her cheeks, her mind racing with conflicting thoughts. She loved Viktor, more than she had ever thought possible. But the choice before her wasn't just about love—it was about her identity, her soul, and the life she had imagined for herself.

Could she really give that up?

"I need time," Lila said finally, her voice trembling. "I need time to think about this."

Viktor nodded, though the sadness in his eyes was unmistakable. "Take all the time you need. I'll be here, whatever you decide."

Lila looked at him, her heart breaking at the sight of the man she loved caught between his desire to protect her and his respect for her choices. She knew that no matter what she decided, there would be consequences. Staying human meant living with the constant threat of death, but becoming a vampire meant losing the very essence of who she was.

The night stretched on in silence, and as Lila stood by the window, watching the rain fall outside, she couldn't shake the feeling that her world was slipping away from her, piece by piece.

And in the shadows of her heart, the question loomed larger than ever:

Could she embrace the darkness for love, or would her humanity be the one thing she couldn't give up?

# Chapter 18: The Rival Clan's Challenge

The night was eerily quiet, as if the world itself was holding its breath. Lila stood at the edge of the safe house's rooftop, the cold breeze whispering across her skin as she stared into the endless expanse of dark sky. The city below was cloaked in shadow, and the weight of the decision she had been wrestling with pressed down on her chest. Viktor had given her the time and space she needed to think about his offer—the chance to become like him, immortal and bound by blood—but the choice was tearing her apart.

Her humanity was all she had ever known, and giving it up felt like losing a piece of her soul. Yet, the love she had for Viktor was undeniable, and the bond they shared only grew stronger with each passing day. It was a love that defied the rules of both their worlds, and she knew that staying human in Viktor's world meant living in constant danger.

But before she could make her decision, the shadows were about to grow even darker.

Footsteps sounded behind her, and Lila turned to find Viktor approaching, his expression tense and guarded. She could feel his anxiety through their bond, a faint hum of unease that prickled at the edges of her consciousness. Something was wrong.

"What is it?" Lila asked, her voice barely above a whisper.

Viktor's gaze shifted to the horizon, his jaw clenched. "We've been challenged."

Lila's heart skipped a beat. "Challenged?"

"By the Crimson Shadows," Viktor replied, his voice tight with anger. "Their leader, Damian, has issued a formal challenge—a duel. He wants to settle this once and for all."

Lila's stomach twisted at the mention of Damian. Viktor had told her about him—a ruthless vampire with ambitions for power, one who wouldn't hesitate to destroy anything or anyone who stood in his way.

The Crimson Shadows had been after them for weeks, and now, it seemed, Damian had found the perfect opportunity to strike.

"Why now?" Lila asked, her voice trembling. "What does he want?"

Viktor's eyes darkened, and for a moment, his control slipped, revealing the depth of his rage. "He knows about you. He knows that you're my weakness."

Lila's breath caught in her throat. "Your... weakness?"

Viktor took a step closer, his gaze locking with hers. "He's using you, Lila. He knows that if he challenges me, if he threatens you, I'll have no choice but to face him. He's counting on the fact that my love for you will cloud my judgment, make me vulnerable."

Lila's heart raced as the gravity of the situation hit her. This wasn't just about a rivalry between vampire clans—it was about her. Damian had discovered the one thing that could bring Viktor to his knees: his love for her.

"But you can't fight him," Lila said, her voice filled with panic. "He'll use this against you. He'll use me."

Viktor's jaw tightened, and she could see the inner conflict raging behind his eyes. "I don't have a choice. Damian is threatening more than just us—he's threatening everything. If I don't accept the challenge, he'll come for you, for anyone we care about. This isn't just a fight—it's a message."

Lila's chest tightened with fear. She knew how dangerous Damian was, and the thought of Viktor facing him alone made her stomach churn with dread. "What if you lose?"

Viktor's gaze hardened, but his voice remained steady. "I won't lose."

Lila swallowed hard, her heart pounding. She had seen Viktor fight before, knew his strength and skill, but Damian wasn't just any vampire. He was powerful, cunning, and willing to do whatever it took to win. And Lila knew that if Damian had issued the challenge, it meant he had a plan—a way to exploit Viktor's love for her.

"Isn't there another way?" Lila asked desperately. "Can't we run? Hide?"

Viktor shook his head, his expression grim. "This isn't something we can run from. Damian won't stop until one of us is dead. And if I don't accept the challenge, he'll see it as weakness, and that will only embolden him. He'll come after you, after anyone he thinks will hurt me."

Lila's breath came in shallow gasps as the full weight of the situation settled over her. This wasn't just about survival—it was about Viktor's honour, about protecting their bond and everything they had built together. But the thought of Viktor risking his life for her, of facing Damian alone, terrified her.

"There has to be something we can do," Lila whispered, tears welling in her eyes. "I don't want to lose you."

Viktor stepped closer, his hand gently cupping her face as his eyes softened. "You won't lose me, Lila. I'll fight for you, for us. I've faced worse than Damian before. But I need you to trust me."

Lila's heart ached at the tenderness in his voice, at the love she could feel radiating from him. But it didn't erase the fear, the gnawing dread that something terrible was about to happen. She didn't want him to fight, didn't want him to risk everything for her.

But Viktor was right—this wasn't just about them anymore. Damian was playing a game of power, and if Viktor didn't fight, the consequences would be far worse.

"When is it?" Lila asked quietly, her voice trembling.

"Tomorrow night," Viktor replied, his hand slipping from her face. "The duel will take place at the old cathedral, just outside the city. It's neutral territory."

Lila nodded, her stomach churning with anxiety. Tomorrow. It felt too soon, too sudden, but she knew there was no avoiding it. Damian wouldn't wait, and neither could they.

"I'm coming with you," Lila said, her voice firmer than she expected.

Viktor's eyes darkened, and he shook his head. "No. It's too dangerous."

"I'm not going to sit back and wait while you fight for me," Lila insisted, her eyes locking with his. "I need to be there, Viktor. I need to see what happens."

Viktor's expression softened, but the worry in his eyes remained. He knew how much this meant to her, but the thought of her being anywhere near the fight made him tense.

"Fine," he said after a long pause, his voice filled with reluctance. "But you'll stay out of harm's way. You can't interfere, no matter what happens."

Lila nodded, though her heart was pounding in her chest. She didn't know what tomorrow would bring, didn't know if she was ready to witness the brutality of a vampire duel. But she knew one thing for certain: she couldn't let Viktor face this alone.

The hours leading up to the duel passed in a blur. Lila couldn't sleep, couldn't eat. Her mind was consumed with worry, her heart aching with the fear of losing Viktor. Every time she closed her eyes, she saw Damian's cruel smile, heard his taunting voice as he used her to manipulate Viktor.

And then, as the moon rose high in the sky, it was time.

The old cathedral stood in ruins, its stone walls crumbling under the weight of time. The wind howled through the broken windows, and the scent of decay clung to the air. It was a place of death, of ancient battles long forgotten, and now it would bear witness to another.

Viktor stood at the center of the cathedral's hollowed nave, his stance firm and unyielding. Lila watched from the shadows, her heart racing as she tried to steady her breath. Every muscle in her body was tense, her hands trembling with anticipation.

And then, from the darkness, Damian emerged.

He moved with the grace of a predator, his eyes gleaming with malice as he approached Viktor. His smile was cruel, a twisted expression of amusement as he sized up his opponent.

"I was wondering if you'd actually show," Damian sneered, his voice dripping with arrogance. "I suppose love really does make you weak."

Viktor's expression remained unreadable, but Lila could feel the tension radiating off him, the barely controlled fury that simmered just beneath the surface.

"This isn't about love," Viktor said coldly. "It's about power. And you'll regret underestimating mine."

Damian laughed, a hollow, mocking sound that echoed through the empty cathedral. "We'll see, won't we?"

Lila's breath caught in her throat as the two vampires squared off, the air around them crackling with tension. She knew what was about to happen would change everything.

And as the first blow landed, the fight for their future began.

# Chapter 19: Love in the Moonlight

The duel had been brutal. Every clash between Viktor and Damian had echoed through the cathedral, reverberating in Lila's bones as she watched from the shadows, her heart pounding with fear and desperation. She had never seen Viktor fight like that before—ferocious, unyielding, and yet graceful. His love for her, his need to protect her, had fuelled every strike. And when Damian had fallen, defeated and humiliated, Viktor had stood victorious, though the weight of the battle lingered heavily in his eyes.

But the fight wasn't over—not truly. Damian's defeat had bought them time, but Lila knew that the Vampire Council was still a threat, still waiting for the right moment to tear them apart. And the darkness of Viktor's world, with all its dangers and betrayals, loomed over them like a shadow.

Yet, despite the tension and the fear, something had changed between them. As the moon rose high in the sky that night, casting its silver glow over the ruins of the cathedral, Lila felt the bond between her and Viktor grow stronger, more undeniable. The battle had proven that their love—though fraught with danger—was something powerful, something worth fighting for.

After the duel, Viktor had brought her back to a secluded safe house nestled in the woods, far from the prying eyes of the Council and their enemies. The moonlight filtered through the trees, casting soft beams of light across the quiet clearing, and the gentle rustle of the wind through the leaves was the only sound that broke the silence of the night.

Lila stood by the window, staring out at the full moon, its pale light bathing the forest in a silvery glow. Her heart was still racing from the events of the day, from the fear of losing Viktor, from the relief of seeing him standing tall after the fight. But now, in the quiet of the night, another emotion bubbled to the surface—desire.

The bond between them had always been strong, but tonight, it felt different. More intense, more raw. It was as if the moon itself had awakened something inside her, something primal and untamed. She could feel Viktor's presence behind her, his energy pulling her toward him even before she turned to face him.

He stood at the edge of the room, his eyes dark and intense as they met hers. There was no need for words—she could feel what he was thinking, could sense the longing in his gaze, the same desire that had been building inside her.

Without a word, Viktor crossed the room, his movements slow and deliberate. The air between them crackled with tension, a pull that neither of them could resist. Lila's breath caught in her throat as he stopped in front of her, his hand gently cupping her face, his thumb brushing lightly across her cheek.

"Lila," he whispered, his voice low and filled with emotion. "I don't want to lose you."

Her heart ached at the vulnerability in his voice, at the raw intensity of the emotions that hung between them. "You won't lose me," she whispered back, her voice trembling. "Not tonight."

Viktor's gaze darkened, his eyes searching hers as if trying to hold on to the moment, trying to savour every second. He leaned in slowly, his lips brushing softly against hers, and the kiss sent a wave of warmth flooding through Lila's body. It wasn't like any kiss they had shared before—it was deeper, more desperate, filled with all the things they hadn't said.

The world outside faded away as they melted into each other, their bond pulling them closer, binding them together in ways that went beyond words. Viktor's hands slid down her arms, his touch sending shivers through her as he pulled her closer, his body pressing against hers.

Lila's heart raced as her hands found their way to his chest, her fingers tracing the lines of his muscles as she felt his heartbeat beneath her palms. He was solid, real, and in this moment, all the fears and doubts that had plagued her seemed to vanish. There was only Viktor, only the man she had fallen for, the man who had risked everything to protect her.

Viktor's lips trailed down her neck, his breath hot against her skin, and Lila let out a soft sigh as her body responded to his touch. Every kiss, every caress, ignited a fire inside her, a need that she couldn't deny. The bond between them pulsed with energy, wrapping around them like an invisible thread, pulling them deeper into each other.

As the moonlight streamed through the window, casting silver beams across their bodies, Lila felt the weight of the world slip away. In Viktor's arms, she felt safe, cherished, and for the first time in a long time, she felt completely free.

Their movements became more urgent, their kisses more heated, as the night deepened. Viktor's hands moved to her waist, lifting her as if she weighed nothing, and he carried her to the bed, their lips never breaking apart. Lila's pulse quickened, her body aching for him, her mind spinning with desire.

When they finally collapsed onto the bed, tangled in each other, the intensity of their connection left her breathless. Viktor's eyes locked with hers, and for a moment, time seemed to stand still. She could see the love in his gaze, the passion, but also the fear—the fear of losing her, of what their future might hold.

But in this moment, none of that mattered. They had each other, and for tonight, that was enough.

As their bodies moved together, Lila felt the full force of their bond, the deep connection that tied them together. It wasn't just physical—it was something far more profound. The love they shared, despite the danger, despite the darkness, was something that transcended the chaos of Viktor's world.

And as the moonlight bathed them in its glow, Lila knew that no matter what the future held, no matter how dark the road ahead might be, this moment was theirs.

When the night finally gave way to dawn, and the first rays of sunlight began to peek through the trees, Lila lay in Viktor's arms, her heart full and her mind at peace for the first time in weeks. She could feel the steady rhythm of his heartbeat beneath her, a reminder of the life they had fought so hard to protect.

Viktor kissed the top of her head, his arms wrapped tightly around her, as if he never wanted to let go. And in that moment, Lila knew that, despite the looming threats and the uncertainty of the future, they had something powerful—something that couldn't be broken.

The full moon had risen and fallen, and with it, they had shared a night that cemented their bond in a way that nothing else could. They had faced danger together, and now, they had found love in the moonlight, a love that would carry them through whatever was to come.

# Chapter 20: A Forbidden Ceremony

The air inside the hidden chamber was thick with an ancient, almost sacred energy. Lila stood at the center of the room, her heart racing as the weight of what she and Viktor were about to do settled over her like a heavy cloak. The chamber itself was deep beneath the old cathedral, concealed from the prying eyes of both the Vampire Council and their enemies. It was a place few knew existed, and fewer still dared to enter.

Tonight, it would become the setting for something forbidden—something powerful.

Lila's breath came in short, nervous gasps as she glanced around the dimly lit room. The walls were made of rough stone, etched with symbols and runes that seemed to hum with an energy she couldn't quite explain. Flickering candlelight cast long shadows across the floor, and the faint scent of incense filled the air. It was a space steeped in ritual, in ancient traditions older than she could comprehend.

In the center of the chamber was a stone altar, low and unassuming, but it held an undeniable significance. This was where the ceremony would take place—the forbidden Bloodbound ritual that would officially link her and Viktor together in a way that went beyond the bond they already shared. It would tie their lives and destinies together, permanently.

Viktor stood beside her, his presence both grounding and intense. His dark eyes, filled with resolve and tenderness, watched her carefully, as if he could sense the uncertainty that gnawed at her. He had explained the ceremony to her, told her what it would mean. But even with that knowledge, Lila felt the gravity of the moment pressing down on her.

This wasn't just about love. This was about something far more dangerous. It was about fate, about binding herself to Viktor's world in a way that could never be undone. Once they completed the ceremony, their connection would be absolute—deeper than even the

Bloodbound bond that had already tied them together. They would be inseparable, their fates entwined for eternity.

"Are you sure about this?" Viktor asked softly, his voice barely more than a whisper as he stepped closer, his hand gently brushing against hers.

Lila looked up at him, her heart pounding in her chest. She could see the concern in his eyes, the way he was giving her one last chance to back out. But she knew, deep down, that there was no turning back—not for her, not for them. She had already made her choice.

"I'm sure," she whispered, though her voice trembled slightly.

Viktor's expression softened, and he nodded, though the tension in his jaw remained. He was worried—worried about what this ceremony would mean, about the danger it would bring. But he had also told her that this was the only way to truly protect their bond, to ensure that neither the Council nor the Crimson Shadows could exploit it. The Bloodbound ceremony was forbidden for a reason—it granted power, but at a cost.

The cost of their freedom, of their destinies, forever entwined.

Lila took a deep breath, trying to steady herself as she prepared for what was to come. She had come so far since meeting Viktor—she had faced death, betrayal, and the constant threat of danger. But nothing had shaken her as much as the thought of losing him. And this ceremony—this ritual—was the only way to ensure that they would never be separated, no matter what the world threw at them.

"Once we begin, there's no going back," Viktor said, his voice filled with both warning and promise. "Our souls will be bound, Lila. We'll share everything—our strength, our pain, our fates. Are you ready for that?"

Lila nodded, her heart full of emotion. "I'm ready."

Viktor held her gaze for a long moment before stepping back slightly, signalling to the figure standing at the far end of the room. A hooded figure—an old vampire elder, sworn to secrecy—emerged from the shadows, their presence ancient and commanding. They were one of the few who still knew the ancient rites, the forbidden ceremonies that even the Council dared not speak of.

The elder approached the altar, their movements slow and deliberate, as if they carried the weight of centuries on their shoulders. Without a word, they placed a small, ornate dagger on the stone surface, the blade glinting in the candlelight. It was simple but elegant, etched with runes that seemed to pulse with a faint energy of their own.

"This ceremony is forbidden," the elder said, their voice low and raspy. "But its power is undeniable. Once it is complete, your souls will be bound for eternity. What one feels, the other will feel. What one suffers, the other will suffer. Your fates will be linked in ways that go beyond life and death."

Lila's pulse quickened as she listened, the magnitude of the ritual becoming all too real. She had already felt the effects of the Bloodbound bond in small ways—feeling Viktor's presence, sensing his emotions. But this ceremony would take it to another level, linking their very souls.

Viktor stepped forward, standing beside the altar, and motioned for Lila to join him. She moved slowly, her heart racing as she approached, her eyes fixed on the dagger that would soon draw their blood.

"Place your hands on the altar," the elder instructed, their voice filled with the weight of tradition.

Lila's hands trembled as she placed them on the cool stone, her skin prickling with the energy that seemed to radiate from the altar itself. Viktor did the same, his hands brushing against hers as they both steadied themselves for what was to come.

The elder lifted the dagger, the blade gleaming ominously in the flickering light. "With this cut, your blood will mix, and your souls will bind. From this moment forward, you will be one."

Lila's breath caught in her throat as the elder brought the dagger to Viktor's palm, making a shallow cut across his skin. Blood welled up, dark and rich, and without hesitation, the elder moved to her, repeating the action on her palm. The sharp sting of the blade was brief, but the sight of her own blood mingling with Viktor's was a shock to her system.

"Let the blood of the Bloodbound unite," the elder intoned, their voice resonating through the chamber. "By the ancient rites, I bind your souls, your fates, your lives."

The elder pressed Lila's palm to Viktor's, and the moment their blood mixed, a surge of energy shot through her. It wasn't just a physical sensation—it was something deeper, something primal. She could feel Viktor's presence more acutely than ever before, as if he were a part of her. Their emotions, their thoughts, seemed to swirl together, intertwining in a way that left her breathless.

Her heart pounded, and she could feel Viktor's heartbeat mirroring her own, the rhythm of their lives now beating in unison. The bond between them, once a tether, now felt like an unbreakable chain, pulling them closer, locking them together.

Lila gasped, overwhelmed by the intensity of it all. She could feel Viktor's emotions flooding into her—his love, his fear, his need to protect her. And she knew, in that moment, that he could feel hers too. The walls between them had crumbled, and they were truly, irrevocably bound.

The elder stepped back, their task complete. "It is done."

Lila turned to Viktor, her eyes wide as she tried to process what had just happened. The bond between them pulsed with a life of its own, and she could feel every thought, every emotion he had, as if they were her own.

"Viktor," she whispered, her voice trembling with awe.

Viktor reached out, pulling her into his arms, and the connection between them deepened even further. His touch sent a wave of warmth through her, and she knew that whatever challenges lay ahead, they would face them together. Bound by blood, by soul, by love.

"I'm yours," Viktor whispered, his lips brushing against her ear. "Now and forever."

Lila closed her eyes, her heart swelling with emotion. "And I'm yours."

The night stretched on, and as the candles flickered in the ancient chamber, Lila and Viktor stood together, their lives now intertwined in ways that neither of them could ever undo.

They had crossed the line into the forbidden, and there was no turning back.

# Chapter 21: The Blood War

The sky was a deep, oppressive grey as war descended upon the vampire world. Lila stood on the edge of the battle, her heart pounding in her chest, watching in horror as the conflict between the vampire clans unfolded before her eyes. It had begun with the Crimson Shadows and Viktor's defiance of their leader, Damian, but now, the battle had escalated into something far larger—a full-scale war between the clans, with blood and power on the line.

It wasn't just about territory anymore; it was about survival.

The tension that had been simmering between the rival clans for centuries had finally boiled over, and Viktor, as one of the few vampires willing to defy the Vampire Council, had become a target. His leadership of the rebel faction, those vampires who refused to bow to the Council's control, had made him a key figure in the unfolding war. And now, with Lila by his side, their Bloodbound bond had made them both powerful—and vulnerable.

Lila had never imagined her life would come to this: standing on the edge of a battlefield, watching as vampires clashed in the shadows, their movements too fast for her human eyes to fully comprehend. The sounds of snarls, the clash of fangs and claws, and the sharp hiss of steel echoed in the distance, creating a symphony of violence and chaos.

She had always known that Viktor's world was dangerous, but nothing could have prepared her for the reality of a full-scale vampire war. And now, despite the ceremony that had bound their fates together, she felt powerless—trapped in the middle of a conflict she barely understood, yet completely tied to.

Viktor stood at her side, his presence a steadying force in the midst of the storm. His dark eyes scanned the battlefield, calculating, strategizing, but Lila could feel the tension radiating off him. She knew he was worried—not just for the outcome of the war, but for her.

Their bond had deepened after the forbidden ceremony, and now, every emotion, every fear, felt amplified between them.

"You need to stay here," Viktor said, his voice calm but filled with urgency. "I can't risk you being out there."

Lila's heart clenched at his words. She understood the danger, knew that if she stepped into the battle, she would be vulnerable. But she also knew that Viktor was walking into the heart of the conflict, and the thought of him fighting alone—of losing him—was unbearable.

"I don't want to hide," Lila said, her voice trembling with emotion. "I want to help."

Viktor's gaze softened as he looked at her, but his resolve didn't waver. "I know. But this isn't your fight, Lila. It's mine."

"Because of me," she whispered, guilt tightening her chest. "This all started because of us."

Viktor shook his head, stepping closer and gently placing his hands on her shoulders. "No. This war was coming long before you and I ever met. The Council, the Crimson Shadows—they've been hunting power for centuries. We're just the latest excuse. But I won't let them use you against me."

Lila bit her lip, trying to hold back the tears that threatened to spill over. She hated feeling like a liability, hated that her very presence put Viktor in more danger. But at the same time, she couldn't bear the thought of standing on the sidelines, helpless, while the man she loved fought for his life.

"Please, just be careful," she whispered, her voice breaking.

Viktor's expression softened further, and he leaned in, pressing a gentle kiss to her forehead. "I will. I promise."

He pulled away, and Lila watched as he turned and began to make his way toward the battlefield, his steps measured and purposeful. Her heart ached as she watched him go, knowing that with every step he took, he was walking into danger. The bond between them pulsed with energy, and she could feel his determination, his fear—his love.

As Viktor disappeared into the shadows, joining the other vampires who were preparing for battle, Lila stood frozen in place, her mind racing. She wanted to follow him, to stand by his side and fight, but she knew that Viktor was right—this wasn't her fight. Not directly.

But she couldn't stand by and do nothing.

With a deep breath, Lila turned away from the battlefield and hurried back toward the camp where Viktor's faction had gathered. The rebel vampires who followed him were a diverse group—vampires from various clans who had grown tired of the Council's iron-fisted rule. Many of them had been wary of Lila at first, unsure of what to make of a human among their ranks, but after the Bloodbound ceremony, they had come to accept her as part of their world.

As she made her way through the camp, Lila spotted a familiar face—Serena, one of Viktor's most trusted allies and a fierce warrior in her own right. Serena's sharp eyes met Lila's as she approached, and the vampire nodded in acknowledgment.

"You shouldn't be here," Serena said, though there was no malice in her voice. "It's about to get ugly out there."

"I know," Lila replied, her voice steady despite the fear gnawing at her insides. "But I can't just sit back and watch. I want to help."

Serena raised an eyebrow, her expression curious. "You're human. There's only so much you can do."

"I know I can't fight like you," Lila admitted, "but there has to be something. Anything."

Serena studied her for a moment, her expression unreadable. Then, with a nod, she motioned for Lila to follow her. "Come on. There might be something you can do."

Lila followed Serena through the camp, her heart pounding with anticipation. She didn't know what she could offer in a world of vampires, but she refused to be a bystander. She would find a way to contribute—to make sure Viktor knew she was with him, even if she couldn't fight by his side.

As they reached a small group of vampires gathered around a large map of the area, Serena turned to Lila. "These are our strategists," she explained. "They've been mapping out the battlefield, tracking the movements of the enemy clans. Information is just as important as strength in a war like this."

Lila's eyes widened as she took in the detailed map, the markers showing the positions of various vampire factions. "So, what do I do?"

Serena pointed to a spot on the map, a location that appeared to be a weak point in the Crimson Shadows' defences. "You can help relay information. We've got messengers running back and forth between the battlefield and the command center. It's dangerous, but it's vital. If you're up for it, you could be one of them."

Lila's heart raced, but she nodded without hesitation. "I'll do it."

Serena's expression softened slightly. "You're braver than I thought."

With that, Lila joined the team of messengers, her heart pounding with both fear and determination. It wasn't the front lines, but it was something. And as she began her first run, darting through the shadows with information that could turn the tide of the battle, she knew that, in her own way, she was fighting for Viktor—fighting for them.

The night stretched on, and the sounds of battle grew louder, more intense. Lila lost track of how many times she ran between the camp and the battlefield, her mind focused on the task at hand. But with every run, her connection to Viktor pulsed stronger, and she could feel the strain of the fight on him—the weight of the war bearing down on his shoulders.

And then, as dawn began to break, a sudden surge of pain shot through the bond, sending Lila stumbling to the ground. Her heart raced, her breath coming in ragged gasps as she clutched her chest, feeling Viktor's pain as if it were her own.

Something had gone wrong.

Without thinking, Lila pushed herself to her feet and sprinted toward the battlefield, her mind filled with panic. She had to find him. She had to know he was okay.

The scene before her was chaos—vampires locked in brutal combat, blood staining the ground, the air thick with tension. But Lila didn't care about any of that. Her eyes searched the battlefield, desperately seeking Viktor.

And then she saw him.

Viktor was standing at the center of the fray, his body battered and bloodied, but still standing. But he was surrounded—Crimson Shadows closing in on him, their leader Damian, who had somehow survived, at the head of the pack.

Lila's heart raced as she watched the scene unfold, her fear turning into a raw, primal need to protect Viktor. She had come so far, endured so much, and she wasn't about to lose him now.

"Viktor!" she screamed, her voice cutting through the noise of the battlefield.

Viktor's head snapped in her direction, and the moment their eyes met, something shifted between them. The bond pulsed with energy, a surge of power that Lila had never felt before. It was as if the Bloodbound ceremony had awakened something within her—something stronger than either of them had realized.

And as the Crimson Shadows descended on Viktor, Lila ran toward him, ready to fight by his side, no matter the cost.

The Blood War had begun, and there was no turning back.

# Chapter 22: Escape into Darkness

The air was thick with the scent of blood and the lingering echoes of battle as Lila and Viktor fled the battlefield. The Crimson Shadows and rival vampire clans had descended upon them, overwhelming their forces and leaving them with no choice but to retreat. Lila's heart pounded in her chest, her breath coming in shallow, panicked gasps as they sprinted through the dense forest, the sounds of pursuit ringing in the distance.

They had won the skirmish, but the war was far from over.

Viktor moved with the speed and grace of a predator, his senses heightened as he guided Lila through the underbrush. His body was still bruised and bloodied from the battle, but he never faltered, his focus entirely on getting her to safety. Lila, however, could feel the weight of the night pressing down on them—every crack of a twig, every whisper of the wind sent a jolt of fear through her. Their enemies were closing in, and they were running out of time.

"Keep moving," Viktor urged, his voice low but filled with urgency.

Lila didn't need to be told twice. She pushed herself harder, her muscles burning with exhaustion, but she refused to slow down. She knew what would happen if they were caught—what the Crimson Shadows and the Vampire Council would do to them. There would be no mercy, no chance of escape.

Their enemies were relentless, hunting them not just for the Blood War, but for their bond. The forbidden Bloodbound ceremony had marked Lila and Viktor as targets—something both sides wanted to exploit. Lila's very existence had become a threat to the delicate balance of power in the vampire world, and now, she and Viktor were paying the price.

The trees closed in around them, the darkness deepening as they ventured deeper into the forest. The moonlight barely filtered through the dense canopy, casting eerie shadows across the ground. Lila's heart raced, her senses heightened by fear and adrenaline. Every sound felt amplified, every breath a reminder of the danger that lurked just beyond the trees.

"We're almost there," Viktor said, his voice strained but steady. "There's a safe house ahead. We'll regroup there."

Lila nodded, though her mind was spinning with doubt. They had been running for what felt like hours, and though she trusted Viktor's instincts, the constant threat of being hunted gnawed at her. Their enemies were everywhere—Crimson Shadows on one side, the Vampire Council on the other. They were trapped between two warring forces, and no matter how far they ran, there was always the sense that they were being watched, followed.

The tension between them had grown heavier since the battle, their bond strained under the weight of their constant flight. Viktor was distant, his focus entirely on survival, but Lila could feel his frustration simmering beneath the surface. He blamed himself—she could sense it through their bond. He blamed himself for bringing her into this, for not being able to protect her from the dangers of his world.

But Lila didn't blame him. She had chosen this life—chosen to stay by his side, no matter the cost. Still, the fear and uncertainty hung over them like a dark cloud, and she couldn't shake the feeling that their enemies were closer than they realized.

As they neared the safe house, Viktor slowed, his hand reaching out to stop Lila. His eyes scanned the surroundings, his senses alert. "Wait."

Lila froze, her breath catching in her throat as she listened for any sign of danger. The forest was eerily silent, but she could feel the tension in the air, the sense that something—or someone—was watching them.

"What is it?" Lila whispered, her voice barely audible.

Viktor's jaw tightened, his eyes narrowing as he continued to scan the area. "We're not alone."

Lila's heart raced, her mind flashing back to the battle, to the faces of the vampires who had hunted them relentlessly. She had hoped they had outrun them, but deep down, she knew that hope had been a fleeting one. Their enemies were too powerful, too determined to let them slip away so easily.

Before she could respond, the sound of movement echoed through the trees—footsteps, faint but unmistakable. Lila's pulse quickened, and she instinctively moved closer to Viktor, her fear spiking.

"They're close," Viktor muttered, his voice low but filled with tension.

Without another word, Viktor grabbed Lila's hand and pulled her toward the thickest part of the forest. They moved swiftly, weaving through the trees, their footsteps barely audible as they slipped deeper into the shadows. But Lila knew that their pursuers were closing in. The Crimson Shadows and the Council wouldn't rest until they had both Viktor and her in their grasp.

As they ran, Lila's mind raced with thoughts of escape, of survival. How long could they keep running? How long could they stay ahead of their enemies before exhaustion, or worse, betrayal, caught up with them? The weight of the Bloodbound bond pulsed between them, reminding her that their destinies were now tied together. But even that bond couldn't protect them from the dangers that surrounded them.

They reached a small clearing, and Viktor stopped abruptly, his body tense as he listened for any sign of their pursuers. The silence was deafening, and for a moment, Lila dared to hope that they had escaped.

But then, out of the shadows, a voice cut through the night.

"You can't run forever, Viktor."

Lila's blood ran cold at the sound. She recognized the voice—it was Damian, the leader of the Crimson Shadows. The very vampire Viktor had defeated in battle, now back for revenge.

Viktor's eyes darkened, his body going rigid as he stepped in front of Lila, shielding her from the threat. "Damian," he growled, his voice laced with fury. "You're still alive."

Damian emerged from the shadows, his smile cold and calculating. "You didn't think it would be that easy, did you? Killing me isn't something just anyone can manage."

Lila's heart pounded as she watched the two vampires square off. She had seen firsthand how dangerous Damian was, and the thought of him coming after Viktor again sent a wave of dread crashing over her.

"You've made a mistake, Damian," Viktor said, his voice calm but deadly. "This war isn't over yet."

Damian's smile widened, his eyes gleaming with malice. "No, but it will be soon. And when it is, you'll be nothing more than a memory."

Without warning, Damian lunged at Viktor, his movements impossibly fast. Viktor met him head-on, the clash of their bodies sending a shockwave through the clearing. Lila stumbled back, her heart racing as the two vampires fought with a ferocity she had never seen before. Fangs bared, claws slashing, they were a blur of motion—each strike more brutal than the last.

Lila's hands trembled as she watched the fight, her fear for Viktor's life twisting her insides. She wanted to help, to do something, but she knew that getting involved would only make things worse. Viktor needed to focus on the fight—on keeping them both alive.

But even as Viktor fought with everything he had, Lila could feel the weight of their enemies closing in. The Crimson Shadows weren't the only ones hunting them. The Council was out there too, waiting for their moment to strike, and Lila knew that it was only a matter of time before they were caught in the crossfire.

The fight between Viktor and Damian raged on, but Lila could sense Viktor's exhaustion. He had been fighting for too long, running for too long, and Damian knew it. He was playing the long game, wearing Viktor down with each strike.

And then, with a savage blow, Damian sent Viktor crashing to the ground, his body limp and bloodied.

"Viktor!" Lila screamed, her voice filled with panic as she rushed toward him.

But Damian was faster. He grabbed her by the arm, pulling her away from Viktor, his grip like iron. Lila struggled, fear clawing at her as she tried to break free, but Damian's strength was overwhelming.

"You see, Lila," Damian whispered, his voice cold and triumphant, "this is what happens when you align yourself with weakness."

Lila's heart pounded in her chest, terror surging through her as she looked into Damian's cruel eyes. She knew what was coming, knew that Damian was moments away from ending Viktor's life. But just as Damian raised his hand, preparing to deliver the final blow, a flash of movement caught his attention.

Viktor, battered and bloodied, had risen to his feet.

"You won't touch her," Viktor growled, his voice filled with a raw, primal fury.

And in that moment, Lila saw the depth of Viktor's love for her—the power of their bond. He wasn't fighting just for survival; he was fighting for her.

With a burst of energy, Viktor launched himself at Damian, their bodies colliding in a violent clash that sent them both tumbling into the darkness. The forest echoed with the sound of their struggle, but this time, it was Viktor who had the upper hand.

And as Damian finally fell, defeated and broken, Lila rushed to Viktor's side, her heart pounding with relief and fear.

"We need to go," Viktor said, his voice rough and strained. "We're not safe here."

Lila nodded, her heart still racing as she helped Viktor to his feet. The weight of the night, the fear, the exhaustion—it all threatened to overwhelm her, but she knew they couldn't stop now.

Their enemies were still out there, closing in.

And the darkness was their only escape.

# Chapter 23: The Council's Verdict

The grand hall of the Vampire Council was a place that radiated power and intimidation. Its ancient walls were lined with towering stone columns, etched with runes of forgotten languages, and the air was thick with the weight of centuries of judgment. Lila stood beside Viktor in the center of the chamber, her heart pounding in her chest as she looked up at the gathered vampires who made up the Council. Their eyes gleamed with cold detachment, their faces emotionless as they prepared to pass judgment on the most forbidden of acts: Viktor's Bloodbound bond with a human.

The trial was about to begin.

Viktor stood tall beside her, his expression unreadable but his presence a steady source of strength. His body, still healing from the brutal battle with Damian and the Crimson Shadows, bore the marks of his recent fight. But here, in the Council's chamber, it was not his physical strength that would be tested—it was his will, his defiance of vampire law, and, most importantly, the love he and Lila shared.

Lila's heart tightened as she looked at the Council, seated in a semicircle of shadowed thrones high above them. Each member was a powerful vampire, ancient and feared. They had the authority to pass judgment on all vampire-kind, and no one dared question their rulings. They held absolute power, and today, they would decide her and Viktor's fate.

The leader of the Council, a vampire named Aldric, sat in the center, his face severe and cold. His piercing eyes bore down on Lila and Viktor, as if he could see into their very souls. He had ruled the Council for centuries, and his word was law.

"You stand accused of violating the most sacred of vampire laws," Aldric began, his voice echoing through the chamber. "The Bloodbound bond between a vampire and a human is forbidden, as it threatens the balance of power in our world. Viktor, you have not only violated this law, but you have openly defied the Council's authority by refusing to sever the bond."

Lila swallowed hard, her hands trembling at her sides. She knew the gravity of what they were facing—knew that if the Council found them guilty, there would be no escape. The bond they had fought so hard to protect could be their undoing.

Viktor's gaze never wavered as he stepped forward, his voice calm but filled with defiance. "The bond between Lila and me is not a threat. It is love. And I will not apologize for loving her."

A murmur rippled through the Council at Viktor's words, their disapproval palpable. Aldric's eyes narrowed, and he leaned forward slightly, his gaze fixed on Viktor.

"Love?" Aldric said, his tone mocking. "You have allowed your emotions to cloud your judgment, Viktor. The Bloodbound bond is a danger to our kind. It gives humans too much power over us, weakens our control, and makes us vulnerable. You know this."

"The bond does not make us weak," Viktor argued, his voice rising. "It makes us stronger. Lila is not a threat. She is a part of me now, and I would die before letting anyone harm her."

Lila's heart swelled at Viktor's words, but fear twisted in her chest. She knew the Council cared little for love or emotion. They cared only for power and control, and to them, the bond between a vampire and a human was a direct challenge to their authority.

Aldric's expression darkened, and his voice turned cold. "You speak of strength, yet you have defied the very laws that hold our society together. Your bond with this human is a rebellion against everything we stand for."

Viktor's jaw clenched, and Lila could feel his anger simmering beneath the surface. But before he could respond, another voice spoke up—a Council member seated to Aldric's right, a vampire named Selene. She was younger than most of the others, but her power was undeniable. Her silver eyes gleamed as she regarded Lila and Viktor with interest.

"Viktor, you claim that your bond makes you stronger," Selene said, her tone measured. "But what proof do you offer? The Bloodbound bond is unstable at best, dangerous at worst. It ties two beings together in ways that can lead to destruction. How can we trust that this bond will not unravel and bring ruin to us all?"

Viktor turned to Selene, his voice steady but filled with conviction. "Because the bond between Lila and me is more than just a connection of blood. It is love. And love—true love—is stronger than any law, stronger than any force that seeks to tear it apart."

Lila's breath caught in her throat as she listened to Viktor speak. His words were filled with passion, but she knew that love alone might not be enough to sway the Council. They needed more. They needed to prove that their bond was not a threat, but a strength.

Steeling herself, Lila stepped forward, her voice trembling but clear. "The bond we share is not something we chose lightly," she said, her eyes moving across the faces of the Council members. "But it's something we've fought for, something we've bled for. We didn't ask for this bond, but now that we have it, we won't turn our backs on it."

Aldric's gaze shifted to her, and Lila could feel the weight of his scrutiny. "You are human," he said coldly. "You have no place in our world. Your existence threatens everything we have built."

Lila's hands balled into fists, her fear momentarily overshadowed by anger. "I may be human, but I'm not weak," she shot back. "I've faced more danger in the past few weeks than I ever thought possible, and I've stood by Viktor's side through it all. I'm not asking to be part of your world—I just want to live. We just want to be together."

The chamber fell into a tense silence as the Council members exchanged glances, clearly unsettled by Lila's defiance. Viktor reached for her hand, squeezing it gently, his touch grounding her in the midst of the storm.

Aldric stood, his towering presence casting a long shadow over the room. "Enough," he said, his voice carrying the weight of finality. "You have defied the laws of our kind, Viktor. The Bloodbound bond you have created is a dangerous precedent, one that cannot be allowed to continue. The Council must decide if you are fit to live among us—or if your rebellion will cost you your lives."

Lila's heart skipped a beat, her breath catching in her throat. This was it—the moment of truth. She could feel Viktor's grip tighten on her hand, his tension mirrored in their bond. If the Council ruled against them, there would be no escape. They would be executed, their love deemed too dangerous to exist.

The Council members fell into hushed discussion, their voices too low for Lila to hear. Every second felt like an eternity, and the weight of their fate pressed down on her with suffocating intensity. She had never felt so helpless, so vulnerable. All she could do was wait, and pray that Viktor's words—his love—had been enough.

After what felt like an eternity, Aldric raised his hand, silencing the room.

"The Council has reached a verdict," he announced, his eyes cold and unforgiving. "Viktor, your defiance of the law is undeniable. You have created a bond that should never have existed, and you have placed our entire world at risk by doing so."

Lila's stomach churned with fear, her heart pounding in her chest as she braced herself for the worst.

"However," Aldric continued, his tone measured, "the Council recognizes the strength of your bond. Though we do not condone your actions, we cannot deny the power it holds. For this reason, we have chosen to spare your lives—on one condition."

Lila's breath hitched, her mind spinning with the possibilities. What condition?

"You will sever the bond," Aldric declared, his voice firm. "You will dissolve the Bloodbound connection between you, or you will face execution. The choice is yours."

Lila's world tilted as the words sank in. Sever the bond? Their bond, the very thing that had brought them together, the thing that had kept them alive? How could they sever it and still be together?

Viktor's grip on her hand tightened, and she could feel the turmoil raging within him. He had fought so hard to protect their bond, to keep them connected. Now, they were being asked to destroy the very thing that had defined them.

"We can't do that," Viktor said, his voice trembling with barely restrained fury. "We won't."

Aldric's expression remained unmoved. "Then you will die."

Lila's heart raced, her mind spinning with panic. She didn't want to lose Viktor, didn't want to lose the bond they had fought so hard to protect. But the Council had left them with an impossible choice: sever the bond and live, or keep it and die.

Tears welled in her eyes as she looked up at Viktor, her voice barely a whisper. "What do we do?"

Viktor's gaze softened, and he leaned down, pressing his forehead to hers. "I won't lose you," he whispered, his voice filled with emotion. "Not like this."

The chamber fell into silence once again, the weight of their decision hanging over them like a sword. They were trapped, caught between love and survival, between the bond that defined them and the life they had fought to protect.

And as the Council watched, waiting for their answer, Lila knew that whatever they chose, nothing would ever be the same.

# Chapter 24: The Betrayal Within

The night was colder than usual, the sky above Viktor and Lila's temporary sanctuary clear and starless. They had escaped the Vampire Council's verdict, but the tension between them was palpable, every unspoken word weighed down by the impossible choice they now faced. Sever their Bloodbound bond and live, or keep it and risk death. It was a decision neither of them had been ready to make, and now, in their fragile hiding place deep in the forest, the uncertainty lingered like a storm on the horizon.

The safe house, hidden among towering trees and surrounded by a thick mist, was known only to Viktor's most trusted allies. It was a place they had retreated to before when danger loomed too close, and it had always served as a refuge. But tonight, the air felt different, charged with an unfamiliar unease that set Lila on edge.

She sat by the window, staring out at the darkened forest, her thoughts spinning in a constant cycle of fear, doubt, and the inescapable pull of her bond with Viktor. The choice the Council had given them seemed designed to tear them apart—an impossible test of their love, their loyalty, and the power that connected them.

Viktor had been quieter than usual, his mind clearly weighed down by the consequences of the Council's ultimatum. He had told Lila that they would find a way, that they wouldn't be forced into the Council's trap, but as each day passed, the pressure mounted. They were running out of time, and their enemies were still closing in.

A soft knock on the door pulled Lila from her thoughts, and she turned to see Viktor enter the room, his face unreadable as he crossed the space to stand beside her. His dark eyes were filled with worry, and Lila could sense his turmoil through their bond, a constant echo of the fear and doubt she herself carried.

"How are you holding up?" Viktor asked softly, his voice tinged with exhaustion.

Lila gave him a small, strained smile. "I'm not sure how to answer that."

Viktor sighed, running a hand through his hair. "I know. I feel it too."

He sat beside her, his hand reaching out to take hers. The warmth of his touch grounded her, but the heaviness in his expression made her heart ache. This wasn't the life she had imagined for them—not this constant fear, not this never-ending fight for survival.

"We're going to figure this out," Viktor said quietly, his voice filled with determination. "I won't let the Council tear us apart."

Lila nodded, though the doubt still gnawed at her. They had survived so much already—battles, betrayals, the Council's trial—but this felt different. The threat was more insidious, more dangerous because it was coming from within. Their very bond, the thing that had given them strength, was now the source of their greatest vulnerability.

"I know," Lila whispered. "But it feels like we're running out of time."

Before Viktor could respond, there was a knock at the door—sharp and urgent. Both Viktor and Lila tensed, their senses immediately on high alert. Viktor rose swiftly, his expression hardening as he moved toward the door. He opened it to reveal Serena, one of his most trusted allies and the only other vampire in his inner circle who knew the location of their hideout.

Serena's face was pale, her eyes wide with worry. "Viktor, we have a problem."

Viktor stepped aside, allowing her to enter. "What is it?"

Serena glanced at Lila briefly, then back at Viktor. "There's been a leak. Someone within our ranks—someone close to us—has betrayed us. The Crimson Shadows know where you are. They're coming."

Lila's heart plummeted as the words hit her. A betrayal. From within. The very people they had trusted with their lives had turned against them, and now, their enemies were closing in.

Viktor's expression darkened, his jaw tightening as the weight of Serena's words sank in. "Who?"

Serena hesitated, her eyes flickering with uncertainty. "I don't know exactly who, but the information is spreading fast. Someone fed the Crimson Shadows everything they need to track you down."

Viktor cursed under his breath, his fists clenching at his sides. Lila could feel his anger simmering beneath the surface, the betrayal cutting deep. They had been so careful, so deliberate in choosing who to trust, and yet, it hadn't been enough.

"How much time do we have?" Viktor asked, his voice sharp.

"Not long," Serena replied, her tone grim. "We need to leave before they get here. If we don't, they'll find you—and the Council won't be far behind."

Lila's pulse quickened, her fear spiking as she glanced at Viktor. He was already moving, grabbing a bag and quickly packing their essentials. "We need to go," he said, his voice firm but laced with frustration. "Now."

As Lila hurried to gather her things, her mind raced with questions. Who had betrayed them? How had the Crimson Shadows gotten so close? The thought that someone from Viktor's inner circle—someone who had stood by them through so much—could have turned against them was terrifying. It wasn't just about survival anymore; it was about trust, about the people they relied on to stay alive.

Minutes later, they were moving swiftly through the forest, the safe house already far behind them. The night was dark, the shadows thick and suffocating, but they couldn't afford to slow down. Every second felt like a countdown, the weight of the betrayal pressing down on them as they fled.

Viktor's hand never left Lila's, his grip tight as he led her through the woods. She could feel the tension radiating off him, the frustration and anger at being forced into yet another flight for their lives. But beneath it all was something deeper—something more painful. The betrayal had shaken him in ways Lila hadn't expected, and she could sense the toll it was taking on him.

"Do you think Serena's right?" Lila asked as they ran, her voice breathless. "Do you think someone close to us sold us out?"

Viktor didn't answer right away, his jaw clenched as they moved through the trees. When he finally spoke, his voice was low and filled with anger. "I don't want to believe it, but it's the only explanation. Someone fed the Crimson Shadows everything they needed to find us."

Lila's heart ached at the thought. She had seen Viktor's loyalty to his people, his dedication to protecting those he cared about. The idea that someone within his trusted circle could have turned on him—it was a betrayal that cut deeper than any wound.

"But who?" Lila pressed, her mind racing. "Who could do something like this?"

Viktor's eyes darkened, and his voice was filled with a quiet fury. "That's what I intend to find out."

They continued through the forest, their breath coming in ragged gasps as they pushed forward. But even as they ran, Lila couldn't shake the feeling that their enemies were closing in, that the betrayal had set in motion something far more dangerous than they could anticipate.

As they reached a clearing, Viktor stopped suddenly, his eyes scanning the area. His body tensed, and Lila followed his gaze, her heart sinking.

A figure stood at the edge of the clearing, cloaked in shadow.

It was someone they both knew.

Lila's breath caught in her throat as the figure stepped forward, revealing themselves in the pale moonlight.

It was someone from Viktor's inner circle.

The betrayer.

The one who had sold them out.

And as the realization hit her, Lila's blood turned to ice.

"Why?" Viktor's voice was barely more than a growl, his eyes locked on the traitor.

The vampire standing before them—one they had once trusted—smiled coldly, their eyes gleaming with malice. "Because, Viktor, love makes you weak. And weakness in our world is deadly."

Lila's heart pounded in her chest as the reality of their situation crashed down on her. The betrayal had come from within, and now, they were standing face-to-face with the one who had set everything in motion.

And in that moment, she knew that their love—the very thing that had brought them together—was now the weapon their enemies would use to destroy them.

# Chapter 25: A Dangerous Proposition

The safe house had been compromised. The betrayal from within Viktor's trusted circle had shattered the fragile sense of security that Lila and Viktor had been clinging to. They had barely escaped with their lives, fleeing into the night once again, and now, as they took refuge in a remote cave deep in the mountains, the weight of the situation pressed down on them like a suffocating fog.

Lila sat by the fire they had hastily built, her mind racing as she tried to make sense of everything that had happened. The betrayal had shaken them both, but it was the uncertainty of what lay ahead that gnawed at her. The Crimson Shadows were hunting them, the Vampire Council was closing in, and now, they didn't even know who they could trust. Viktor was on edge, pacing back and forth near the cave's entrance, his every movement tense and deliberate.

The silence between them was thick, filled with unspoken fears and doubts. The Council's ultimatum—sever the bond or face execution—loomed over them, and Lila could feel the strain it was placing on Viktor. He had always been her protector, her shield in the dangerous world of vampires, but now, they were running out of options.

As the fire crackled in the quiet of the cave, the soft sound of footsteps echoed from the shadows. Lila tensed, her heart racing as she looked up, expecting danger. Viktor's head snapped toward the entrance, his body immediately going on high alert. But what stepped into the flickering firelight was not an enemy.

It was Selene.

The younger Council member, who had spoken out during their trial, appeared almost ghostly as she approached. Her silver eyes gleamed in the dim light, and though her posture was relaxed, Lila could sense the weight of something more behind her expression.

"Selene?" Viktor growled, stepping between Lila and the vampire. "What are you doing here?"

Selene held up her hands in a gesture of peace, her voice calm but laced with urgency. "I'm not here to fight, Viktor. I'm here because I have something to offer."

Lila's heart skipped a beat as she watched the two vampires face off. Selene had been one of the few Council members who hadn't seemed entirely hostile during the trial, but Lila still didn't trust her. The Council's motives were always murky, and Selene was no exception.

Viktor's eyes narrowed. "You've already made your decision. The Council wants our bond severed."

"Yes," Selene agreed, her gaze flickering toward Lila. "But I didn't agree with Aldric's methods. The Council doesn't see the full picture, Viktor. They fear your bond, but they're blind to what it truly represents."

Lila shifted uncomfortably, her mind spinning with questions. Why was Selene here? What did she want?

"Then why are you here?" Viktor asked, his voice hard. "What are you offering?"

Selene took a step closer, her eyes locking onto Lila's. "I've come with a proposition for Lila."

Lila's breath caught in her throat, a sense of dread pooling in her stomach. "A proposition?"

Selene nodded, her expression serious. "The Council is closing in, and your bond with Viktor is a threat they won't tolerate. But there's another way to protect yourself—to ensure your survival."

Viktor stiffened, his hand tightening into a fist at his side. "What are you talking about?"

Selene's gaze never wavered as she spoke. "Lila, you're caught between two worlds—human and vampire. The Council sees your humanity as a weakness, something that makes Viktor vulnerable. But there's a way for you to leave that weakness behind. If you become one of us, you'll gain the protection you need. The Council won't see you as a threat anymore, and the Crimson Shadows won't be able to use your humanity against Viktor."

Lila's heart raced as the meaning behind Selene's words sank in. She was offering her the chance to become a vampire, to leave her human life behind and step fully into Viktor's world. It was a proposition that promised protection, power, and the ability to stand by Viktor's side without fear of being used as leverage.

But at what cost?

Viktor's reaction was immediate. He stepped forward, his voice filled with anger and disbelief. "You can't be serious. You think turning her into one of us will solve everything? You're asking her to give up her humanity."

Selene's expression remained calm, but there was a flicker of something darker in her eyes. "I'm not asking her to do anything. I'm giving her a choice. The Council's decision is final, Viktor. If you keep this bond intact, they will come for you both. But if Lila chooses to become one of us, she will gain the protection of the Council."

Lila felt as if the ground had been ripped out from beneath her. The choice that Selene was presenting was monumental—leave behind her humanity and become a vampire, or stay as she was and continue to be hunted, caught in a cycle of danger that threatened both her and Viktor. It was a way out, but it wasn't a choice she had ever imagined facing.

She glanced at Viktor, searching his face for guidance, but his expression was a mixture of fury and pain. He didn't want this for her—he didn't want her to feel forced into a decision that would change her life forever. And yet, the reality of their situation was impossible to ignore.

"Why would you offer this?" Lila asked, her voice trembling. "Why are you helping us?"

Selene's gaze softened, and for the first time, there was a hint of something more—something almost human in her expression. "Because I see what the Council refuses to. Your bond is different. It's not a weakness. But you won't survive long enough to prove that if you remain as you are."

Lila's pulse quickened as the weight of the decision pressed down on her. Become a vampire. Leave behind everything she had ever known—her family, her past, her humanity—and join Viktor in a world of darkness, of immortality. It was a way to protect them both, but the cost was staggering.

Viktor stepped closer to her, his eyes filled with emotion. "You don't have to do this, Lila. Don't let her pressure you into something you're not ready for."

Lila's heart ached at the conflict in his voice. She knew he would never ask this of her, never push her into a decision that would rob her of her humanity. But the truth was, the danger wasn't going away. The Council, the Crimson Shadows—they would never stop coming for them. And Selene's offer was a way to end the chase, to take control of her fate.

But at what cost?

"I'm not ready," Lila whispered, her voice breaking. "I don't know if I can do this."

Selene's eyes gleamed with understanding, but there was a sense of finality in her tone. "You don't have much time. If you choose to remain human, the Council will hunt you down. You'll never be free."

Lila's heart pounded in her chest, torn between the life she had known and the love she had found with Viktor. She wanted to be with him, wanted to fight for their bond, but the idea of losing herself—losing everything that made her human—was terrifying.

The fire crackled between them, the flickering light casting long shadows across the cave. Viktor reached for her hand, his grip firm but filled with love. "Whatever you choose, I'm with you. Always."

Tears welled in Lila's eyes as she looked at him, the man who had given up so much to protect her. But this choice—this decision—was one she had to make on her own.

She turned to Selene, her voice barely a whisper. "I need time."

Selene nodded, though there was a sense of urgency in her gaze. "Time is running out, Lila. Choose wisely."

With that, Selene turned and disappeared into the shadows, leaving Lila and Viktor alone in the cave, the weight of her proposition hanging heavy in the air.

Lila stared into the fire, her mind spinning. The choice before her was impossible. Stay human and continue to be hunted, or leave behind everything she had ever known and become a vampire. Either way, their lives would be changed forever.

And as the fire flickered in the darkness, Lila knew that whatever decision she made, there would be no going back.

# Chapter 26: The Power of Blood

The night was heavy with tension as Lila sat by the fire, her thoughts swirling around Selene's proposition. The weight of the choice—whether to remain human or to become a vampire—pressed on her, but another, deeper shift was stirring within her, one that had been growing ever since the forbidden Bloodbound ceremony.

She could feel it now, more than ever: a strange, new energy humming through her veins, an awareness that hadn't been there before. At first, it had been subtle—a heightened sense of Viktor's presence, an ability to anticipate his emotions, to feel his pain. But recently, it had become more intense, more powerful, as if her very blood was changing, responding to the bond in ways she didn't fully understand.

As Lila stared into the flickering flames of the fire, she realized with a sudden clarity: her bond with Viktor was evolving, granting her abilities she had never thought possible.

She shifted uneasily, trying to shake off the unease that came with this realization, but the truth was undeniable. The bond was more than just an emotional or spiritual connection—it was transforming her, and she had no idea how far it would go. And worse, if she could feel it, others could too.

Viktor, sitting across from her, noticed the change in her demeanour. His dark eyes narrowed with concern as he leaned forward. "Lila? What's wrong?"

Lila bit her lip, unsure of how to explain the strange sensations coursing through her. She had told Viktor about the small changes she'd noticed, but this was different. The power now surging within her felt more pronounced, more dangerous.

"I don't know," she admitted, her voice shaky. "It's the bond... I can feel it growing. It's not just emotions anymore, Viktor. It's something else, something... physical."

Viktor's expression darkened, and he moved to sit beside her, his presence steadying but filled with an undercurrent of worry. "What do you mean, physical?"

Lila hesitated, unsure of how to put her experience into words. "It's like I can feel your strength, your power. I'm... changing. And it's not just in my head—I can feel it in my body, in my blood."

Viktor's jaw clenched, and he took her hand in his, his touch grounding her as she struggled to understand what was happening. "This is the Bloodbound connection," he said, his voice filled with both awe and concern. "It's more than just a link between us—it's merging our strengths. But this... this shouldn't be happening to you, not like this."

Lila's heart raced as she processed his words. She knew that the Bloodbound bond was powerful, but she had never expected it to manifest in such a physical way. Her humanity should have prevented her from experiencing the full extent of the bond's power, but now, it seemed that the lines between human and vampire were blurring.

"What does this mean?" Lila whispered, her voice trembling. "Am I... turning into something else?"

Viktor shook his head, his eyes filled with uncertainty. "No. You're still human, Lila, but the bond is changing you in ways neither of us anticipated. This kind of connection is rare—almost unheard of. It's drawing power from me, but it's also amplifying it in you."

Lila's pulse quickened as the implications of Viktor's words sank in. She wasn't just linked to Viktor anymore—she was becoming something more, something that defied the laws of their worlds. And if Viktor could sense it, then others could too.

Before Lila could respond, a sudden chill swept through the cave, and Viktor's body tensed. His hand tightened around hers as his eyes darted to the entrance. He wasn't alone in feeling it. Lila felt the cold, too—a presence, dark and oppressive, lurking just beyond the cave's mouth.

"We're not alone," Viktor muttered, his voice a low growl.

Lila's heart leaped into her throat as shadows shifted near the entrance, and a figure stepped into the firelight. It was a vampire, one Lila had never seen before, but there was an unmistakable air of power and menace surrounding him. His eyes, dark and predatory, fixed on Lila with an intensity that made her blood run cold.

Viktor rose to his feet, positioning himself between Lila and the intruder. "Who are you?" he demanded, his voice low and dangerous.

The vampire smiled coldly, his gaze never leaving Lila. "You're not the one I came for, Viktor."

Lila's breath caught in her throat as the vampire's attention remained fixed on her, his eyes gleaming with something she couldn't quite place—curiosity, hunger, and something darker, more insidious.

"The girl," the vampire continued, stepping closer. "She's the one. I felt it—her power. The bond has awakened something inside her, something rare. She's no longer just a human."

Lila's pulse raced as the weight of his words sank in. He knew. He could feel it—the same power that had been growing inside her, the power that had come from her Bloodbound bond with Viktor.

"What do you want with her?" Viktor growled, his body tense, ready to fight.

The vampire's smile widened, revealing a flash of sharp fangs. "You have no idea what you've created, do you? A human bonded to a vampire with such strength? She's a weapon—a weapon that others will covet."

Lila's blood ran cold as the realization hit her. This vampire, whoever he was, wasn't the only one who had noticed the changes in her. Others would come for her too, seeking to use her newfound power for their own ends.

"You think you can take her?" Viktor's voice was filled with fury, his posture defensive. "I'll tear you apart before you lay a hand on her."

The vampire laughed, a low, menacing sound that echoed through the cave. "Oh, Viktor, you misunderstand. I'm not here to fight you. I'm here to offer her protection."

Lila's stomach twisted at the vampire's words. Protection? From whom? And at what cost?

The vampire's gaze flickered to her again, his voice softening as he spoke directly to her. "You're powerful now, Lila. More powerful than you know. But that power comes with a price. The Council, the Crimson Shadows—they will all come for you. They'll see you as a threat, as a tool to be used. But I can help you. I can teach you to control your abilities, to use them for your own protection."

Lila's heart raced as the vampire's words sank in. He was offering her a way out—a way to harness the power that had been growing inside her, to protect herself from the threats closing in around her. But she couldn't shake the feeling that there was something more, something darker, lurking beneath his offer.

"What's the price?" Lila asked, her voice barely a whisper.

The vampire's smile returned, cold and calculating. "Your loyalty. You'll belong to me, Lila. I'll teach you to control your power, but in return, you'll serve me. Together, we'll rise above the Council, above the Crimson Shadows. No one will be able to touch you."

Lila's heart pounded in her chest, torn between fear and the undeniable pull of the power that had been growing within her. She didn't want to be used, didn't want to be a pawn in someone else's game. But the threat was real, and this vampire was right—her connection to Viktor had made her a target.

Viktor stepped forward, his eyes blazing with anger. "She doesn't belong to anyone. And she won't be your weapon."

The vampire's smile faded, and his eyes darkened as he met Viktor's gaze. "You can't protect her forever, Viktor. The power of blood is stronger than you realize. And when others come for her, you won't be enough to keep her safe."

Lila's mind raced, her thoughts spiralling as the weight of the situation pressed down on her. The bond with Viktor had granted her power, but it had also put her in danger—danger that Viktor alone might not be able to protect her from. And now, this vampire, this powerful stranger, was offering her a way to survive.

But at what cost?

As the fire crackled between them, Lila's mind raced with the impossible choice before her. Accept the vampire's offer and gain the protection she needed, or reject him and face the growing threat alone.

And as Viktor stood beside her, ready to fight for her at any cost, Lila realized that the power of blood—her blood—had already changed everything.

# Chapter 27: Bloodline Secrets

The air was thick with tension as Lila sat alone in the small room, the weight of recent revelations pressing heavily on her chest. Viktor had gone out to scout the area, leaving her with time to process everything that had happened. Her Bloodbound connection to Viktor had awakened something within her—something powerful and dangerous—and now, the vampire world had begun to see her as more than just a human.

But it was Selene's words and the mysterious vampire's proposition that haunted her the most. They had both hinted at something deeper, something beyond just the bond with Viktor. There was a hidden strength in her blood, a power that was both a gift and a curse. And the more she thought about it, the more she wondered if there was something she didn't know about herself—something lurking in her past.

Lila's mind raced with questions. Why was the bond affecting her so strongly? Why did the vampires seem so drawn to her, as if she were more than just a human connected to Viktor? There had to be an answer, something more than the Bloodbound ritual alone.

Determined to find answers, Lila began to dig through the few belongings she had brought with her when she and Viktor first fled. Among the items was a small wooden box, something she had taken from her mother's house years ago after she passed away. It contained old photos, documents, and keepsakes from her family, most of which she had never given much thought to.

She had never considered the possibility that her lineage might hold secrets. Her life had always seemed ordinary—until Viktor had come into it. But now, with the strange power coursing through her veins, she couldn't help but wonder if her past held the key to unlocking the mystery of what was happening to her.

As Lila sifted through the contents of the box, her fingers brushed against a faded envelope sealed with a wax stamp. The paper was yellowed with age, the writing on the front in elegant, flowing script. Her heart skipped a beat as she carefully opened the envelope, pulling out a letter that looked far older than anything else in the box.

The words inside were written in the same graceful hand, and as she began to read, Lila's breath caught in her throat.

My dearest Elara,

There are things I have kept from you, things I never wished for you to know. But as you grow older, you may begin to sense the truth, and for that, I must prepare you. Our family is not like others. We are bound by blood—blood that ties us to a world far more dangerous than you can imagine. You must never speak of this to anyone, for if they discover what runs through your veins, you will never be safe.

We are descended from a line of great power, a bloodline that connects us to the vampire world. Your father, though he left long ago, was one of them. This is the truth I have hidden from you. You carry within you the blood of vampires. It is a power that, if left unchecked, will draw others to you—those who seek to use you for their own ends. You must be careful, my child, for our bloodline is both a blessing and a curse.

If you are reading this, it means the time has come for you to know the truth. Trust your instincts, and know that whatever happens, you are stronger than you think. But be wary, for there are those who will seek to control the power you carry.

With love, always,

Your mother.

Lila stared at the letter, her hands trembling. Her mother had known. She had known about the connection to the vampire world, about the power in their bloodline, and she had kept it hidden all these years. But now, as Lila sat in the flickering light of the small room, the pieces of her past began to fall into place.

Her father—someone she had never known—was a vampire. That's why the Bloodbound connection with Viktor had affected her so strongly. It wasn't just the bond itself that was changing her—it was the dormant power in her blood, a power that had been passed down through generations. And now, that power was waking up.

Lila's heart raced as she tried to process the truth. She wasn't just an ordinary human caught up in the vampire world—she was part of it. Her bloodline carried the same ancient power that vampires coveted, and now that it had begun to manifest, there was no telling what it might mean for her future.

Suddenly, everything made sense. The heightened abilities, the way vampires had sensed something different about her, the dangerous attention she had begun to attract—it was all because of her bloodline. She was more than just a human connected to Viktor. She was a descendant of vampires, and that lineage made her both powerful and vulnerable.

Lila's mind raced with possibilities. If she carried vampire blood, did that mean she could become like them without losing her humanity completely? Was there a way to control the power growing within her, or was she destined to be used as a weapon, just as the mysterious vampire had hinted?

As the weight of the revelation settled over her, Lila heard the faint sound of footsteps approaching. Viktor stepped into the room, his eyes immediately locking onto her, sensing the shift in her emotions. He crossed the space quickly, kneeling beside her.

"Lila, what's wrong? What happened?"

She handed him the letter, her heart pounding as he read it. Viktor's expression darkened as he took in the words, his jaw tightening as he pieced together the implications.

"This changes everything," he muttered, his voice low. "Your bloodline... it explains why the bond is affecting you like this. You're not just human. You're connected to our world in a way we never realized."

Lila swallowed hard, her voice barely a whisper. "What does this mean for us?"

Viktor met her gaze, his eyes filled with a mixture of awe and concern. "It means you're far more powerful than we thought. And it means the vampires who've been hunting us... they'll want you even more now."

Lila's stomach churned with fear and uncertainty. She had already felt the pull of the vampire world, the way it had tried to claim her. But now, knowing that she carried the blood of vampires within her, the danger felt even more real.

"They'll come for me," she whispered, her voice trembling.

Viktor nodded, his hand tightening around hers. "Yes. But they won't have you, Lila. I won't let them."

Lila's mind raced, the weight of the secret she had uncovered pressing down on her. She was part of this world now, not just because of Viktor, but because of who she was. The bloodline she had been born into carried a power that could change everything, and now that she knew the truth, there was no going back.

The fire flickered between them, casting shadows across the room as Lila and Viktor sat in the heavy silence. Their bond had brought them together, but now, it was her bloodline that would decide their future. She was no longer just a girl caught in the web of vampire politics—she was part of the web itself.

And as the truth of her lineage settled over her, Lila realized that the greatest battle was yet to come.

# Chapter 28: Battle for the Bloodbound

The air was electric with tension as Lila stood on the edge of the battlefield, her heart pounding in her chest. The darkened sky above was heavy with storm clouds, mirroring the storm brewing between the vampire clans below. This was it—the final confrontation. The battle that would decide their fate. And for the first time, Lila stood not as a bystander, but as a full participant, ready to embrace the dangers of Viktor's world and fight for the bond that had brought them together.

Viktor stood beside her, his eyes scanning the horizon, his jaw set in grim determination. The weight of leadership had settled on his shoulders, and though Lila could feel his inner turmoil, his outward appearance was every bit the powerful leader his clan needed. He had spent years building his forces, gathering vampires who, like him, had rejected the authority of the Vampire Council and the Crimson Shadows. Now, with enemies closing in on all sides, it was time to face them.

But it wasn't just about survival anymore. This battle was about the Bloodbound bond—about Lila and Viktor's forbidden connection and the power it had awakened in her. The truth of her lineage, the vampire blood running through her veins, had changed everything. She wasn't just fighting for Viktor's survival; she was fighting for her own.

The battlefield stretched out before them, a vast expanse of open ground surrounded by jagged cliffs. The wind whipped through the air, carrying with it the scent of blood and the faint echoes of the forces gathering just beyond the horizon. The opposing armies—vampires loyal to the Council, Crimson Shadows hungry for power, and Viktor's own rebel forces—were preparing for war.

Lila's heart raced as she glanced at Viktor, his face hard and unyielding as he spoke to the clan leaders who had come to fight by his side. She could feel the weight of his worry through their bond, the constant pressure of the choices they had made. But there was also something else—a fierce determination, a love that had only grown stronger with every battle they had faced together.

"You don't have to do this," Viktor said, turning to face her, his voice low but filled with intensity. "You can stay back, where it's safer."

Lila shook her head, her resolve firm. "No, Viktor. I'm with you. I've made my choice, and I'm not running anymore."

Viktor's gaze softened as he reached out, gently cupping her face in his hands. "I don't want to lose you."

Lila placed her hand over his, her eyes meeting his with equal intensity. "You won't. We're in this together."

The bond between them pulsed with energy, a tangible reminder of the connection they shared. It wasn't just about love anymore—it was about survival. The Bloodbound bond had given them strength, but it had also made them a target. The Council wanted to sever it, the Crimson Shadows wanted to use it, and now, Lila's newfound power made her a prize to be fought over.

As the tension mounted, a low, rumbling sound echoed through the air—the unmistakable approach of their enemies. Viktor turned toward the sound, his body tensing as the figures of the Crimson Shadows emerged from the distant treeline. Led by Damian, the vampire leader who had sworn to destroy Viktor and claim Lila for his own, the Shadows moved like a dark tide across the battlefield, their numbers vast and menacing.

Behind them, the forces of the Vampire Council were not far off, a cold and calculating presence, led by Aldric. They came not to fight for justice, but for control, their eyes set on destroying Viktor's rebellion and severing the Bloodbound bond that defied their laws.

Lila's pulse quickened as she watched the two opposing forces converge, knowing that this battle would be unlike anything they had faced before. But she wasn't afraid. Not anymore. She had come to accept the power growing inside her, the vampire blood that connected her to this world. And though she had once feared it, she now saw it as a source of strength.

Viktor stepped forward, addressing his clan, his voice carrying over the growing wind. "Tonight, we fight not just for our survival, but for our freedom! The Council seeks to control us, to dictate how we live, who we love, and what we fight for. But we are stronger together. We fight for each other. We fight for our future!"

A roar of agreement rose from the assembled vampires, their loyalty to Viktor unwavering. Lila could feel their energy, their commitment to the cause, and it gave her hope. They weren't just an army—they were a family, bound by a shared vision of a world free from the oppressive rule of the Council.

As Viktor's forces prepared for battle, Lila found herself standing beside Serena, the fierce warrior who had become one of Viktor's most trusted allies. Serena's silver eyes gleamed with anticipation, her posture tense but ready.

"You've come a long way," Serena said, her voice low but filled with respect. "I didn't think you'd still be standing here after everything."

Lila smiled, though the weight of the moment pressed heavily on her. "Neither did I. But I'm not going anywhere."

Serena nodded, a hint of admiration in her gaze. "Good. We're going to need that fire in you tonight."

The sound of the approaching armies grew louder, and Lila's heart pounded in her chest as the first of the Crimson Shadows reached the battlefield. Viktor's forces surged forward to meet them, the clash of steel and fangs filling the air as the two sides collided in a brutal, chaotic melee.

Lila gripped the blade Viktor had given her, her pulse quickening as she stepped into the fray. She had never been a fighter, but tonight, everything had changed. She wasn't just fighting for herself anymore—she was fighting for Viktor, for their bond, and for the future they were trying to build together.

The battle raged around her, vampires clashing in a blur of motion and violence. Lila moved with a newfound grace, the power in her blood guiding her movements as she fought beside Viktor. She could feel the bond between them, pulsing with energy, giving her strength even as the fight became more desperate.

Damian's dark figure loomed ahead, his eyes locked on Viktor with a predatory intensity. He had come to finish what he had started, to tear Viktor down and claim Lila's power for himself. But Viktor was ready, his body tense and coiled like a spring as he prepared to face his rival once again.

The two vampires met in a fierce clash, their strikes so fast and powerful that the very air around them seemed to crackle with energy. Lila's heart raced as she watched them, fear and hope warring within her. She knew Viktor was strong, but Damian was relentless, his desire for power driving him to fight with a brutality that threatened to overwhelm them.

But Lila wasn't helpless. She could feel the power of the Bloodbound bond surging within her, amplifying her strength, her senses, her speed. And in that moment, she knew that the bond wasn't just Viktor's strength—it was hers too.

Without hesitation, Lila charged into the fray, her blade flashing as she cut through the enemies that stood between her and Viktor. She could feel the bloodline power in her veins, the strength of her vampire heritage awakening fully as she fought. The world around her seemed to slow, every movement, every strike amplified by the bond she shared with Viktor.

As she reached Viktor's side, Damian turned his cold gaze on her, a cruel smile twisting his lips. "So, the human finally embraces her power. Too bad it won't save you."

Lila's eyes narrowed, her grip on her blade tightening. "I'm not just human anymore."

And with a burst of energy, Lila lunged at Damian, her movements a blur as she struck with the full force of the Bloodbound bond. Damian, caught off guard by her newfound strength, stumbled back, fury flashing in his eyes as he realized what was happening.

The power of her bloodline, combined with the strength of the bond, made Lila more formidable than he had expected.

Viktor, seizing the moment, delivered a brutal strike, sending Damian crashing to the ground. Together, he and Lila stood over their enemy, their bond pulsing with power as they faced the final challenge.

The battle still raged around them, but Lila knew that this moment—this victory—would be the turning point. They had fought for their bond, for their love, and for their place in a world that had tried to tear them apart.

And now, standing side by side, Lila and Viktor knew that nothing could break them.

# Chapter 29: Love Through Blood

The battlefield was a storm of chaos—clashing steel, the furious roar of vampires locked in combat, and the smell of blood thick in the air. Lila fought alongside Viktor, her movements fluid, guided by the power that surged through her veins. She had fully embraced the strength of their Bloodbound connection, and for the first time, she felt like she truly belonged in this world—his world.

But amidst the battle, something went terribly wrong.

It happened so quickly that Lila barely registered the danger until it was too late. She had been fighting her way through a group of Crimson Shadows when she felt it—a sharp, searing pain ripping through her side. She gasped, her knees buckling as she stumbled backward, her vision blurring. Looking down, she saw a blade protruding from her abdomen, coated in her blood.

Time seemed to slow. The sounds of the battle faded away, replaced by the pounding of her heartbeat in her ears. Her body felt cold, her strength ebbing as the darkness crept in.

Viktor's voice broke through the haze, his shout of panic piercing the din of the battle. "Lila!"

He was at her side in an instant, his face pale with horror as he caught her before she collapsed to the ground. Lila's head lolled against his chest, her body limp as she struggled to stay conscious, but the pain was overwhelming, her blood soaking the ground beneath them.

"No, no, no," Viktor muttered, his hands trembling as he pressed them against her wound, trying to stop the bleeding. "Stay with me, Lila. Don't leave me."

Lila's breath came in ragged gasps, her vision swimming as she looked up at Viktor, his face a blur of fear and desperation. She could feel her body shutting down, the warmth of her blood draining away, taking her life with it. It was all happening too fast. The bond that had made her stronger, that had brought them together, was now fading as the darkness threatened to take her.

"I'm sorry," she whispered, her voice barely audible. "I'm so sorry."

Viktor's eyes flashed with panic as he cradled her in his arms. "No. You're not leaving me, Lila. I won't let you."

Lila could barely focus, the world around her fading into a blur of pain and darkness. But through it all, she could still feel him—their bond, pulsing faintly in the back of her mind, tethering her to him. It was weaker now, but it was still there. Viktor was still there.

But she wasn't sure how much longer she could hold on.

"I love you," she managed to whisper, tears slipping down her cheeks. "I love you so much."

Viktor's face twisted with grief, and for the first time, she saw tears in his eyes. "I love you too," he whispered, his voice breaking. "And I'm not going to lose you."

A moment of silence hung between them, the world around them slipping away as Viktor's hands tightened around her. Lila could feel him grappling with an impossible decision—one that she had never imagined they would have to face.

He was a vampire. And she was dying.

Viktor's voice was hoarse as he spoke again, his words heavy with emotion. "Lila, I can save you. But you have to trust me."

Lila's breath caught in her throat, understanding dawning on her as Viktor's meaning became clear. He could save her—by turning her. By making her like him. It was a choice they had avoided, a choice they had both feared. And now, it was the only option left.

Her mind raced, but her body was growing weaker, the pain becoming more distant as her vision dimmed. She was slipping away, and if Viktor didn't act soon, she wouldn't survive.

"Please," Viktor whispered, his voice thick with anguish. "Please let me do this. I can't lose you. Not like this."

Lila stared up at him, her heart breaking at the sight of the man she loved, torn apart by the fear of losing her. The warmth of his hands, the depth of his love—it was all she had left to cling to. She didn't want to die. She didn't want to leave him. But the choice he was offering would change everything.

It would mean giving up her humanity, leaving behind the life she had known. But it would also mean staying with Viktor—forever.

"I... I don't want to leave you," Lila whispered, her voice barely a breath.

Viktor's eyes gleamed with hope, though his expression remained pained. "You won't. I'll keep you with me. Forever."

Lila closed her eyes, tears slipping down her cheeks as she nodded weakly. It was the hardest decision she had ever made, but in her heart, she knew it was the only one that mattered.

"I trust you," she whispered, her voice breaking. "Do it."

Without hesitation, Viktor leaned down, pressing his lips to hers in a kiss that was filled with both desperation and love. He pulled back, his eyes burning with intensity as he whispered, "Hold on, Lila. Just hold on."

And then, with a flicker of hesitation, Viktor lowered his mouth to her neck.

Lila gasped as she felt the sharp sting of his fangs piercing her skin, followed by an overwhelming sensation of warmth flooding through her veins. It wasn't painful—just an intense, consuming sensation, like fire coursing through her. She could feel Viktor's presence all around her, his energy wrapping around her as he pulled her deeper into his world.

The bond between them pulsed stronger than ever, a wave of energy surging through her as Viktor's blood merged with hers, sealing their fates together. It was a strange, dizzying sensation, but in that moment, Lila felt more connected to him than she ever had before.

She wasn't just Lila anymore—she was becoming something else, something more.

Her vision blurred, her body trembling as the transformation began. The pain that had once consumed her began to fade, replaced by a strange, cold clarity. Her heart, once slowing, now raced with a new, unfamiliar energy, and as the darkness receded, she could feel her strength returning.

Viktor pulled back, his eyes searching hers with both hope and fear. "Lila?"

Lila blinked, her senses sharpening as she opened her eyes and met his gaze. The world around her was different—clearer, brighter, more vivid. She could hear the distant sounds of the battle, the rush of the wind, the beating of Viktor's heart. Everything felt... amplified.

"I'm... I'm here," she whispered, her voice stronger than before.

Viktor exhaled in relief, pulling her close and wrapping her in his arms. "You're okay," he murmured, his voice thick with emotion. "You're going to be okay."

Lila clung to him, her heart racing as the reality of what had just happened sank in. She wasn't human anymore. She was like him—a vampire. The transformation had saved her life, but it had also changed her forever.

And as she looked up at Viktor, the man who had given her this second chance, she realized that their bond—the Bloodbound connection—was now stronger than ever.

They had survived. But nothing would ever be the same again.

# Chapter 30: Eternal Love

The first light of dawn was beginning to break over the horizon, casting a soft, pale glow across the battlefield. The storm that had raged through the night had begun to fade, leaving only the remnants of the fierce battle fought between the vampire clans. The air was heavy with the scent of blood, but the fighting had stopped, and the world seemed to hold its breath, waiting for what would come next.

Lila stood at the edge of the battlefield, her senses sharper than ever before. The transformation had changed everything. She could hear the distant rustling of the wind through the trees, smell the earth and the blood beneath her feet, and most of all, she could feel Viktor's presence with a depth that was almost overwhelming. Their Bloodbound connection pulsed between them, stronger than it had ever been, binding them in a way that went beyond love, beyond life itself.

She wasn't human anymore. The moment Viktor had turned her to save her life, she had crossed into his world fully—into the world of vampires. And yet, even as she embraced the cold power flowing through her veins, she knew she hadn't lost herself. She was still Lila, still the woman who had fallen in love with Viktor. But now, she was more than that. She was his equal, his partner, in every sense of the word.

Viktor stood beside her, his dark eyes scanning the horizon, his expression hard but filled with a quiet intensity. He had saved her, given her the chance to live, but in doing so, he had given her so much more. He had given her eternity—a future that stretched out before them, bound together in ways that defied the laws of both human and vampire worlds.

As the light of dawn crept closer, Viktor turned to face her, his gaze softening as their eyes met. He reached out, taking her hand in his, and the warmth of his touch sent a shiver through her. It was strange, she thought—this new awareness of everything, this heightened sense of the world around her—but at the same time, it felt right. It felt like she had always been meant for this.

"How do you feel?" Viktor asked quietly, his voice filled with concern and love.

Lila smiled softly, her heart swelling with emotion as she looked into his eyes. "I feel... alive. More alive than I ever have before."

Viktor's expression softened, a small, relieved smile tugging at the corner of his lips. "I was afraid I would lose you."

Lila stepped closer to him, her hand resting against his chest as she felt the steady rhythm of his heartbeat beneath her palm. "You didn't lose me. You saved me. And now... we have forever."

The weight of her words settled over them both, the enormity of what they had just committed to. Eternity. The very thing they had fought so hard to preserve—their love, their bond—was now permanent, unbreakable. They had faced every challenge thrown at them—battles, betrayals, the Vampire Council's wrath—and emerged stronger because of it.

Viktor's hand slipped around her waist, pulling her close as he rested his forehead against hers. "I never wanted to ask you to give up your humanity," he whispered, his voice filled with emotion. "But I'm selfish, Lila. I couldn't let you go. Not when I had the chance to keep you with me."

Lila tilted her head up, pressing her lips gently to his, the kiss soft but filled with a depth of feeling that went beyond words. When she pulled back, her voice was steady, filled with certainty. "I made the choice, Viktor. I chose you. And I'd make the same choice again, a thousand times over."

A flicker of sadness passed through Viktor's eyes, though it was quickly replaced by a fierce determination. "We'll face the world together now. The Council, the Crimson Shadows, all of it. But we'll be stronger because we're together."

Lila nodded, her hand tightening around his. "Whatever comes, we'll face it. I'm not afraid anymore."

The weight of the battles they had fought—the dangers they had faced—still lingered in the air around them, but the fear that had once gripped Lila's heart was gone. She had been through too much to doubt herself now. The Bloodbound bond had brought her to this moment, had connected her to Viktor in ways she never thought possible, and now, she was ready to embrace whatever came next.

The horizon began to brighten, the sun rising slowly over the distant hills. Viktor's eyes shifted toward the light, his brow furrowing slightly as he looked back at her.

"Daybreak," he muttered, his voice filled with both concern and amusement. "You'll need to adjust to a new schedule now."

Lila laughed softly, the sound of it bright and full of life. "Guess that means no more sunrise walks."

"Not unless we want to turn to ash," Viktor teased, though there was a warmth in his voice that made Lila's heart ache with love.

She stepped closer to him, wrapping her arms around his waist as she leaned against him. "That's okay. I think I've always been more of a night person anyway."

Viktor chuckled, his hand gently stroking her hair as they stood together in the fading darkness. The world around them was quiet now, the battle over, the future uncertain—but they had each other. They had fought for their love, fought to protect their bond, and now they had eternity to enjoy it.

"Eternal love," Viktor whispered, his voice soft but filled with a depth of emotion that sent a shiver through her. "That's what this is."

Lila smiled, her eyes shining as she looked up at him. "Eternal love," she repeated, her voice steady and sure. "And nothing will ever take that away."

The light of the rising sun grew brighter, though it never touched them as they stood in the shadow of the cliffs. The world beyond was still full of challenges—there were still enemies to face, still battles to fight—but none of it mattered in that moment. They had each other, and they had forever.

And as Viktor pressed his lips to hers in a kiss that was filled with both passion and promise, Lila knew that their journey was just beginning. Together, they would face whatever the world threw at them. Together, they would build a future, side by side, as Bloodbound partners—bound by love, bound by fate, bound by blood.

# Chapter 31: The Price of Forever

The moon hung low in the sky, casting a silver glow over the stillness of the night as Lila and Viktor walked through the woods, the silence between them peaceful but filled with unspoken thoughts. It had been weeks since the battle that had nearly torn them apart—since Viktor had made the choice to save her life by turning her into a vampire. The transformation had sealed their fates together, their Bloodbound bond now an unbreakable force connecting them in ways that went beyond anything Lila had imagined.

But with that bond came a new set of challenges, ones that neither of them had fully anticipated. As much as they had longed for eternity together, the world around them hadn't forgotten who they were—or what they had done. And now, as Lila adjusted to her new existence, they both knew that their enemies were regrouping, watching, waiting for the perfect moment to strike.

Viktor's hand tightened around hers as they moved deeper into the forest, his presence steady and reassuring. Lila could feel his love through their bond, the silent strength he offered her at every turn. But even as they walked in the quiet of the night, there was an undercurrent of tension between them, a weight they had both been carrying since the moment she had made the choice to become like him.

She hadn't fully grasped what it meant to live forever—what it meant to leave behind her humanity, her past. The joy of being with Viktor, of sharing this unshakable connection, was overwhelming, but there was also a cost. A price she hadn't yet fully reckoned with.

"Something's on your mind," Viktor said softly, his voice cutting through the stillness of the night. "I can feel it."

Lila glanced at him, her heart swelling at the concern in his eyes. The bond between them was so strong now that she could no longer hide her thoughts, her emotions. Viktor always knew when something was troubling her, and though it brought them closer, it also made it harder to keep her worries to herself.

"I'm just... thinking about everything," Lila admitted, her voice quiet. "About what comes next."

Viktor's expression darkened slightly, his gaze shifting to the path ahead. "You're worried about the Council. And Damian's followers."

Lila nodded, biting her lip. It wasn't just the Council or the remnants of the Crimson Shadows that haunted her thoughts. It was the realization that she had become something new—something that others would fear, covet, or try to destroy. The Bloodbound bond had given her and Viktor strength, but it had also painted a target on their backs.

"We've defeated them before," Viktor continued, his voice filled with quiet confidence. "We can do it again."

Lila wished she could share his certainty, but the weight of eternity pressed down on her in ways she hadn't anticipated. Forever. It was such a long time, and the enemies they had made wouldn't disappear just because they had won a battle. They would come back—stronger, more determined than ever.

"We may have won the battle," Lila said softly, "but the war isn't over."

Viktor stopped walking, turning to face her fully, his hands gently cupping her face. His eyes, filled with love and determination, met hers, and for a moment, the world seemed to still.

"No, it's not," Viktor agreed, his voice calm but firm. "But we're stronger now. Stronger together. I won't let anyone tear us apart, Lila. Not the Council, not the Crimson Shadows. No one."

Lila's heart ached at his words, but she knew it wasn't just about their strength. It was about the choices they had made—the consequences of the bond they had forged. Being Bloodbound wasn't just about love; it was about power, and that power came with a price.

"I'm not afraid of the Council," Lila whispered, her voice trembling slightly. "I'm not afraid of Damian's followers. But forever... it feels so much bigger than I thought it would. I can't help but wonder what we'll lose along the way."

Viktor's eyes softened, and he pulled her closer, resting his forehead against hers. "We'll face it together," he murmured. "Whatever comes, whatever we have to sacrifice, we'll face it side by side."

Lila closed her eyes, letting his words wash over her. She wanted to believe him, to trust that their love, their bond, would be enough to carry them through the eternity they had chosen. But in the back of her mind, there was always the shadow of doubt—the fear that the world wouldn't let them live in peace.

"I never wanted to be a weapon," Lila said quietly, her voice barely more than a whisper. "I never wanted our bond to be something others would use against us."

Viktor's grip tightened around her, and she could feel the tension in his body, the protective instinct rising in him. "You're not a weapon, Lila. You're my partner, my equal. And no one will use you. Not while I'm alive."

Lila smiled softly at his fierce protectiveness, but she knew that wasn't the full truth. The vampire world saw power in their bond, and power always attracted danger. The Council, the Crimson Shadows, other vampire factions—they all saw her as more than just Viktor's partner. They saw her as a symbol, a tool they could exploit. And it scared her.

"We've already seen what the bond can do," Lila said, pulling back slightly to meet Viktor's gaze. "It makes me stronger, but it also makes me vulnerable. And I know others will come for it. For us."

Viktor's expression darkened. "Let them come. We'll be ready."

As much as Lila wanted to believe they could face every challenge, she couldn't shake the feeling that they were standing on the edge of something far bigger than themselves. The vampire world wasn't just going to let them live in peace—not when their bond represented such a threat to the established order.

They had made enemies. Powerful enemies. And now, they had to live with the consequences.

Viktor wrapped his arms around her, pulling her into his embrace. His presence was warm and comforting, and Lila rested her head against his chest, letting herself be soothed by the steady rhythm of his heartbeat.

"We'll find our way through this," Viktor whispered, his voice filled with quiet determination. "Whatever the price, we'll pay it. Because I can't imagine a world without you, Lila. Not anymore."

Lila's heart swelled with emotion, and she closed her eyes, letting the truth of his words settle over her. Whatever challenges lay ahead, whatever dangers they faced, they would face them together. Viktor had saved her life, given her eternity, and she wasn't going to let fear or doubt tear them apart.

"I love you," Lila whispered, her voice soft but filled with certainty. "And I'll face whatever comes with you. Always."

Viktor smiled, pressing a gentle kiss to her forehead. "I love you too."

They stood there in the quiet of the night, wrapped in each other's arms, knowing that the road ahead would be fraught with danger and sacrifice. The price of forever was steep, and their enemies wouldn't rest. But they had each other, and that was enough.

For now, it was enough.

As the first hints of dawn began to break through the trees, Lila and Viktor turned and began walking back toward their hidden sanctuary. The world around them was quiet, but they both knew it wouldn't stay that way for long. The Council, Damian's remnants, and other forces lurking in the shadows would come for them. The price of forever had been paid, but the cost of their love would continue to demand sacrifices.

But as long as they were together, Lila knew they could face it. Bound by blood, bound by love, they were ready to face the world—no matter what it threw at them.

## Disclaimer for Bloodbound Desire

This is a work of fiction. Names, characters, places, and events are either products of the author's imagination or used fictitiously. Any resemblance to actual persons, living or dead, or real events is purely coincidental.

The themes and events in Bloodbound Desire include elements of fantasy, romance, and supernatural occurrences. The depictions of vampires, werewolves, and other paranormal entities are entirely fictional and are not intended to reflect real-world beliefs or practices.

This book contains mature themes, including romance, violence, and suspense, which may not be suitable for all readers. Reader discretion is advised.

The author and publisher are not responsible for any interpretations, actions, or consequences resulting from the reading of this book. All rights are reserved. No part of this book may be reproduced, distributed, or transmitted in any form without prior written permission from the author or publisher, except for brief quotations used in critical reviews or articles.

Milton Keynes UK
Ingram Content Group UK Ltd.
UKHW040715141024
449705UK00001B/65